Protecting Sam

(Sanctuary, Book One)

Abbie Zanders

Protecting Sam

First edition. July, 2018.

Written by Abbie Zanders.

Cover Design: Graphics by Stacy

Cover Image: Eric McKinney, 6:12 Photography

Cover Model: Eric R

Editor: Jovana Shirley, Unforeseen Editing
Editor: C&D Editing
Editor: M.E. Weglarz

ISBN: 1723576670
ISBN-13: 978-1723576676

This book is a work of fiction. Names, characters, places, and incidents either are products of the author's imagination or are used fictitiously. Any resemblance to actual persons, living or dead, events, or locales is entirely coincidental.

Before You Begin

Hi, and thanks for selecting ***Protecting Sam***! Originally, this book was published as part of Susan Stoker's Special Forces: Operation Alpha Kindle World. With the elimination of Kindle Worlds, I'm republishing the story on my own as the first of my new Sanctuary series. Losing the tie to Susan's characters is a bummer, but on the positive side, I can now tie Church's team into my Callaghan world. I think the guys are going to get along very well.

Back-of-book goodness: When you finish reading, check out some of my other titles, too. If you like what you see, please sign up for my newsletter at **https://abbiezandersomance.com**. You'll receive a free ebook and get a chance to win a $25 gift card each month, just for being your awesome military-hero-loving self.

Happy reading!

CHAPTER ONE

~ *Smoke* ~

"Don't look now, Smoke, but I think we're being watched."

Steve Tannen—"Smoke" to his friends—grunted in affirmation. The hairs on the back of his neck had been standing on end from the moment they arrived. He wasn't too worried though. The energy felt more curious and cautious than threatening. He wasn't psychic, not by any means, but his years as a SEAL had honed his instincts, and he knew when he was in someone's sights.

With each haul up the seven flights, he tried to zero in on the source. He was fairly sure it was coming from the apartment next to his; the feeling was strongest each time he passed by.

"Must be a woman," added Hugh "Heff" Bradley—nicknamed after Hugh Hefner for his womanizing ways. "And a pretty one, too."

"Keep it in your pants," Smoke growled.

He didn't want any of Heff's loose ends tripping him up. It seemed no matter where they went, there was some lovesick chick making cow eyes at the former sniper.

Heff liked to claim his dick was a divining rod, an unfailing compass to beautiful, passionate women. Given the number of hot, willing women Heff went through on a regular basis, there might have been a grain of truth to that.

Since Smoke was the one who had to live next to her, Heff would *not* be dipping his wick here. Smoke refused to bear the brunt of the female's inevitable hurt, anger, and/or feelings of rejection when Heff lost interest, as he would after a night or few.

Smoke received an unrepentant grin in response.

"No promises. Isn't there some old disco song about finding heaven on the seventh floor?"

"Cut it out with that disco shit, will you?" groaned Brian "Mad Dog" Sheppard beneath the weight of the box spring. "Disco's dead, man. It died before you were born. Accept it. Move on."

"Never," Heff said on a laugh. "Tony Manero was and always will be my idol."

Regardless, it didn't matter to Smoke if his peeping neighbor was pretty or not. As long as she was quiet, kept to herself, and didn't bother him, they would get along just fine. Smoke preferred to keep the social interaction to a minimum, and he made it a point never to get involved with a woman who knew where he lived. He wasn't a manwhore like Heff, but he wasn't into relationships either. Part of that was due to his transitory lifestyle, but more importantly, he had yet to meet a woman who made him think otherwise. Now at thirty-one years old, he was beginning to accept that might never happen.

Heff had once joked that, when it came to women, Smoke had the emotional range of a pet rock and the charm to match. He wasn't wrong. Despite popular romantic ideals, not everyone was destined for a ball and chain.

Maybe that attitude was part of the problem. He equated serious relationships right up there with punishment.

It wouldn't be like that if you found the right one.

He snorted inwardly. Another worthless romantic ideal. There was no right one, not for him. Women might like the packaging, might like the idea of bagging a SEAL, but they didn't give a lick about *him*. Nor were they willing—or able—to deal with the reality of a man who had looked at things as black or white for so long that he was no longer capable of seeing the grays.

He didn't blame them either. He understood where they were coming from. He had enough trouble keeping his own head on straight; the last thing he wanted was to deal with someone else's baggage, too. And to be responsible for someone else's happiness? That was a great big *thanks, but no, thanks*.

Moving in didn't take long. Smoke didn't have much in the way of possessions. Acquiring things didn't make sense when his life had been more mobile than stationary. The bulk of the last twelve years had been spent in the military, but a smart man knew when it was time to pack it in.

He had killed too many men to count, but he would be damned if he lost one of his own because his sanity had been stretched to the breaking point.

When his old SEAL buddy Matt "Church" Winston had called about his new business venture, Smoke had found himself saying yes … at least for now.

The plan was to convert an old mountain resort into a safe place for vets returning to civilian life, aptly named Sanctuary. Sounded exactly like what he needed. He had forgotten how to be a regular citizen, lost sight of how to play the game and deal with shit by something other than the *any means necessary* mentality that had been drilled into him.

Apparently, it wasn't just him. Lots of others had some issues readjusting, too, which was the whole point of Church's project. Maybe it would work; maybe it wouldn't. Church and Heff, Smoke knew well enough, but the others, not so much. Like any new team, things would shake out over time. Some would stay; some wouldn't. He would reevaluate things and see where he was once Phase I was complete in about six to nine months. In the meantime, he was renting an apartment in town on a month-to-month basis.

He could have bunked with one of the others in the trailers they had on-site, but just the thought of being enclosed in a cramped tin can was enough to give him a case of the sweats.

The village of Sumneyville was only about thirty minutes from the site. It would give him the distance he needed while he got his shit together and started feeling more like a citizen and less like a soldier.

"Looking pretty sparse, dude." This from Nick "Cage" Fumanti as he looked around the mostly empty space.

It *did* look pretty sparse. A brand-new box spring and mattress sat in the lone bedroom. A new recliner sat in the living room along with his new flat screen. The rest consisted of a few boxes of clothes, weapons, and ammo.

The essentials.

There wasn't much sense in acquiring a bunch of stuff he would have to move again in the next couple of months anyway. If he decided to stick around for a while, he would be relocating to staff housing at the resort. And if he didn't, well, he doubted he would be setting down roots in Sumneyville. Until then, this apartment was just a temporary place to set his ass.

For a small-town apartment, it wasn't bad. One of the reasons he had chosen it was because of the many windows and large balcony. Since that last tour, when a cave-in had trapped him underground for sixteen days, he had become partial to open space—and lots of it.

He crossed the room and opened the sliding door to step outside. A deep inhale brought with it the scent of approaching rain and freshly cut grass.

A thick copse of trees separated the building's private parking lot from the well-tended public park beyond with a lit landscaped pathway connecting the two areas. From this height, the mountains surrounding the idyllic valley town were visible. It was a great spot to chill with a couple of cold ones. He made a mental note to pick up a deck chair and a cooler ASAP.

"Nice view." Cage joined him on the balcony, taking it all in.

Smoke knew he was noting escape routes and calculating trajectories. Those things were ingrained in them now, as autonomous as breathing and heartbeats.

"Hello. Is that a pool over there?" Heff asked, appearing between them.

Smoke didn't have to look to know he had spotted the private, fenced-in area off to the right. "Yeah. So?"

"Scenic summer views, man."

Before Smoke could respond, Mad Dog's rough voice rumbled from inside, "Hey, didn't you say something about pizza and beer? All that moving worked up an appetite." The guy was built like a tank, and he was *always* hungry.

Smoke grunted—his version of a laugh—and refrained from pointing out that his lack of worldly possessions had necessitated only two trips.

Seeing as his fridge was empty and the only seating he could offer them was the floor, going out did seem like the best option. He didn't plan on doing much entertaining, nor did he want to encourage guests. Now that he actually had a place of his own, he wanted to enjoy it.

"What's good around here?"

"Franco's is good," Cole "Doc" Watson offered helpfully. "They've got deep dish *and* thin crust, plus plenty on tap."

That sounded good to him.

As Smoke followed them out and locked up, he braced himself for the sensation of being watched again. However, the back of his neck remained prickle-free.

~ *Sam* ~

Samantha Appelhoff quietly untucked her legs and set her tea down, listening as the tread of heavy footsteps passed her door and faded into the stairwell. At least one set belonged to her new neighbor.

Their deep voices had resonated through the

thin drywall. If she had held her ear up to the wall that adjoined their apartments, she might have been able to make out what they were saying, but she wasn't one to pry. Sure, she had watched from her peephole, but that was just practical vigilance. She liked to be aware of her surroundings, and that included who did and didn't belong on her floor.

A key was required to get into the building, but that didn't make it safe. Her last place had had that, too, and that hadn't kept it from being broken into and burglarized. Where there was a will, there was a way, and criminals could be determined.

The ideal, of course, would be to live somewhere with actual security, like a guard or a doorman, but this was a small town. Even if there were a high-security building in the area, it would undoubtedly be beyond her modest price range, especially if she hoped to buy the café where she worked when the current owner retired.

Sam padded on silent feet to the sliding glass door, peering cautiously through the sheer curtains to the private parking lot below. Before long, half a dozen men appeared. She wasn't sure which one was her new neighbor.

All of them walked tall and with the swagger of men confident in their abilities. Probably military, if she had to guess.

Regardless, her new neighbor's past, present, or future was none of her business. She had no intention of striking up a friendship or anything else with him or his friends. As long as he kept the noise down to an acceptable level and stayed out of her way, they would get along just fine.

Two of the men climbed up into a huge flatbed pickup, two into a black SUV with tinted windows, and two into a Wrangler. As if sensing her gaze, the one getting into the driver's side of the Jeep paused and looked up—right at her.

Sam stepped back quickly.

Had he seen her?

No, he couldn't have. She was seven floors up and had been behind the sheers. He was probably looking up to check that he had closed his windows since the darkening sky and the scent of moisture in the air meant a storm was on the way.

It hadn't felt like that though. It was as if he had known she was watching and locked right onto her with eerie accuracy.

Fighting a shiver, she leaned forward again, just in time to see the vehicles pulling out onto the street and heading north.

~ *Anthony* ~

Anthony checked his reflection in the window, smiling at the result. No one would ever recognize him in this getup. He was a human chameleon— able to change his outward appearance at will with clever disguises. He would reveal himself eventually, of course, but not yet.

He wouldn't leave anything to chance this time. Everything had to be perfect.

Each day brought him closer to making her his forever.

He hated that he had scared her, but visiting her home had been necessary. He had needed something of hers. Something intimate. Something recent and personal, so he could fccl close to her until the time was right. Like the simple cotton nightgown he had removed from her hamper that held her scent. He had wrapped it around his pillow so that, when he slept, he could pretend she was next to him. And the embroidered, feminine handkerchief he always kept in his pocket so that, no matter where he was, she was right there with him. It wasn't quite the same as being able to reach out and touch her, but it was something.

Her subsequent relocation had been unexpected and unfortunate, but he had allowed for minor hiccups here and there. She hadn't gone far, and it had been child's play to find her again. His efforts would pay off in the end.

Anthony's steps slowed when he reached the apartment building. Several large men were maneuvering a recliner through the front door. He didn't like the look of them. They carried themselves like arrogant, cocky military assholes who thought they were better than everyone else. Still, he forced a smile and held the door, then slipped in behind them.

Pretending to check his mailbox, he watched out of his peripheral vision as they got the big chair on the elevator. His heart and fists squeezed when the digital display stopped at number seven. *Her* floor.

One of those guys must have taken the empty apartment next to Samantha's. That complicated things.

Anthony turned around and left before they came back down. This was just another test, another challenge to prove he was worthy. And this time, he wouldn't fail.

CHAPTER TWO

~ *Smoke* ~

It wasn't until the next week that Smoke finally got to see what his watchful neighbor looked like, and even then, it was only by chance.

Although he was no longer active duty, his internal alarm clock was still set to zero four hundred. Knowing that efforts to go back to sleep would be unsuccessful, he opted for an early morning run. The sun was still an hour or two from rising, and he always liked the peacefulness before the rest of the world roused and started moving.

He was opening his door the same time she stepped out of hers.

"Morning," he said.

She swiveled around to face him, body tense and eyes alert in a classic moment of fight or flight. Her reaction wasn't quite what he had expected, but he guessed he should have. There was a reason his code name was Smoke. He had mastered the art of stealth, to the point where it was second nature.

It was just another example of how out of touch he was. *Normal people don't like being snuck up on, dumbass.*

He tried to ease some of the tension by not advancing and by offering what he hoped was a friendly smile.

Her gaze took in his trainers, sweats, and tee, mentally gauging the level of immediate threat. Some of her fear receded, but plenty of wariness remained.

Smart woman.

Heff had been right. She *was* pretty. Shiny chestnut hair fell in soft waves just past her shoulders. Big gray-green eyes peered up at him through thick, dark lashes. Delicate but sensual features and dark pink Cupid's bow lips were currently turned down in the hint of a scowl. Black jeans and Chucks revealed nice womanly curves, as did the fitted black polo with the emblem of a local coffeehouse. Well, that explained the predawn rise and shine.

"Morning," she responded quietly.

Positioned between the elevator and the stairwell, she slid her gaze between them and him. He had the distinct impression she would opt for whichever one he didn't take.

He made it easy for her. He turned toward the stairwell.

His analytical brain processed her odd reaction all the way down. Was she normally skittish, or had something happened to make her that way? Couldn't just be him, could it? Yeah, he was a lot bigger than her, but since she didn't top five-three or so and had a petite frame, most people were. More importantly, why did he care?

Regardless of what she might have thought, he was no threat to her. But given the way she had acted, she believed *someone* was.

He tried to shake it off. After all, it was none of his business. Privacy was something he embraced wholeheartedly, and she seemed to value hers. Yet he found himself stalling outside the building anyway to do warm-up ham and calf stretches before his run.

She emerged less than a minute later, hesitating but not stopping as she stepped out onto the sidewalk and saw him. He pretended not to notice her.

The same sensations he had been feeling occasionally ran up and down the length of his spine. They told him two things. One, she was definitely the one who had been watching him. And two, she was watching him now.

She walked hurriedly past him, her fist clutched around something that looked like a set of keys. It proved she was at least thinking of her safety, though there was nothing she could use as an effective defense against someone like him.

She glanced back once or twice as she put distance between them, her gaze constantly swiveling to the front and sides as she moved.

Instead of going into the parking lot, she

continued along the sidewalk. He waited until she disappeared from view, and then he veered toward the park, shaking off the unusually strong urge to follow her.

The early morning air was cool, crisp, and clean, filling his lungs as his feet ate up the miles. He couldn't stop thinking about the way those big gray-green eyes had looked up at him in fear. They had made the innate protector in him sit up and take notice.

He reminded himself that he should be minding his own business. That was what regular guys did, right? Clearly, she was a grown woman, capable of making her own decisions. She hadn't asked for his help, and chances were, she wouldn't appreciate his meddling.

The sun was just coming up when he made it back. He slowed down to a walk, then leaned against the building for another stretch. Once again, skin on the back of his neck prickled, warning him that he was in someone's sights. It felt decidedly different than the curious, assessing glance of his skittish neighbor.

Smoke scanned the parking lot, his eyes catching the image of a man in a nondescript gray sedan. The man appeared to be taking pictures with his cell phone. The moment Smoke spotted him, the guy put the phone down and stared back. It was too far away to get a good look, but something about the guy set off his internal warning system.

As Smoke straightened and started walking toward the vehicle, the guy popped it into reverse, back out of the spot, and took off in a hurry.

Smoke managed to get a make and a partial plate. All the while, his mind told him he was being paranoid, but his gut told him he might have just discovered the reason behind his neighbor's fear.

~ *Sam* ~

"What can I get for you, sir?" Sam asked again, forcing a smile at the jerk standing in front of the counter, talking to someone on his hands-free device. Apparently, *that* conversation was more important than placing his order, aggravating both her and the dozen or so people in line behind him.

When he held up his index finger in a classic *wait* gesture again, Sam took a step to the side and addressed the annoyed-looking woman next in line. "Ma'am? What can I get you?"

"I'll have a large hazelnut, skim, two sugars, and a—"

"Excuse me," the first guy said irritably. "It's my turn."

Sam ignored him. Now, *he* could wait. "And a …" she prompted the woman.

The woman flicked her eyes to the rude guy, then back to Sam. "And a blueberry muffin, please."

"For here or to go?"

"To go, please."

"You got it," Sam said, turning around to fill the order.

"*Excuse me*." The jerk with the phone raised his voice, forgetting his call.

"I'll be with you in a moment, sir."

"No, you'll be with me now. You were waiting on me."

She flicked a gaze his way, unsurprised to find his face red and his expression angry. The quick mental assessment came naturally. *Expensive suit. Latest gadgetry. Hideous power tie. Misplaced sense of superiority. Yep. Jerk.*

"I *was* waiting on you, but you were too busy to tell me what you wanted, and there are others who'd like to get to work on time." Sam bagged the coffee and muffin, turning back to the woman. "That'll be four twenty-three, please."

"Hey, I'm talking to you." The jerk leaned his body over the counter, blocking the woman from paying.

Sam stiffened, drawing herself up to her full, if unimpressive, height. "And I'm telling *you* to back off."

Everyone in the coffeehouse was looking over now, waiting to see what would happen next. Even the hazelnut–blueberry muffin lady stood frozen with a five-dollar bill in her hand.

"I demand to see the manager."

"You're looking at her."

"The owner then."

"Is there a problem?"

The deep, masculine voice drew her attention to the handsome, rugged man speaking and stepping forward from the back of the line. She had been so focused on the rude customer that she failed to notice that her new neighbor had come in. It was unlike her to be so unaware of her surroundings, especially with men like him who seemed to suck the very air from the space around him.

A wave of fresh male deodorant and soap hit her nose, and his hair looked damp around the ends. Clearly, he had showered since his early morning run. His strong jaw was shaven baby smooth, and his faded Levi's and long-sleeved tee showcased hinted at some impressive muscles beneath.

She pushed back the unwanted images of her neighbor—naked under the spray, soaping himself up—before they could take hold.

"No," Sam said right about the same time the asshole said, "Mind your own business, buddy."

Her neighbor stepped closer and glared down at the man. Several inches taller and far broader, he was an imposing sight.

"She *is* my business, and you're not my buddy. Now, apologize to the nice lady and everyone else in line who has had to wait for no good reason. Then, take your very important call and your business elsewhere."

"Not without my—"

Whatever he was about to say faded away when her neighbor's massive hand landed on the asshole's shoulder. "Do I need to repeat myself?"

Those big fingers flexed, and the business jerk winced.

"I'm … sorry," he said to Sam between clenched teeth as he waved vaguely in the direction of the line of customers.

"Now, leave," her neighbor rumbled ominously.

The guy took off, muttering smart remarks the moment he was out of arm's length. Once he was out the door, Sam gaped at her neighbor, who then turned around and took his place at the back of the line again.

"Lucky you," hazelnut-muffin lady murmured.

"I don't … he's not …" Sam shook her head, words failing her. She couldn't explain her new neighbor's surprising claim, nor should she have to. Yes, it had been nice of him to step up like that, but she was no one's business.

When her new neighbor reached the counter, he acted as if nothing unusual had happened. "Coffee, black."

"What size?"

"The biggest you have."

"Anything else?"

"Those muffins look good. Did you make them?"

She blinked. No one had ever asked that before. "Yes."

He nodded. "Then, I'll take two."

"What kind? We have chocolate, blueberry, apple spice—"

"Surprise me."

"For here or to go?"

"For here. Do you get a break?"

She bit her lip, her brain warning her to say no and her sense of propriety saying yes. He *had* come to her defense. His involvement had significantly hastened the jerk customer's departure. The guy probably would have caused more of a fuss otherwise. That deserved a minute of her time and a sincere thank-you. Besides, they were in a well-lit public place, surrounded by people. She was safe— or at least as safe as she could be around a man who looked like he could handle himself in any situation.

"Yeah, in about ten minutes."

He nodded. "I'll wait."

She was keenly aware of her neighbor as she continued to take and fill orders. He didn't stare, not exactly, but she could tell he was checking out and analyzing everyone in the place. To his credit, he ignored the appreciative stares and looks women were giving him, quietly sipping his coffee and eating his muffins, occasionally looking down his phone.

When she could delay no longer, she let Jenna, the part-time college student, take over. Then, Sam wiped her hands on her apron and stepped out from behind the counter.

His gaze immediately swiveled in her direction, and he stood up in a gentlemanly gesture when she approached.

"Sit down," he said in that deep, rumbling voice.

She stiffened immediately. The more she saw of him, the more she was convinced he was military—or at least former military. He had this aura of danger surrounding him, and he was clearly used to issuing orders. White knight or not, she didn't like people telling her what to do.

"Please," he added when she remained standing.

Points to him for being astute and having manners.

She slid into the chair across from him. Best to just get this over with and out of the way.

"Thanks. For before, I mean. But it wasn't necessary. I would have handled it."

He nodded, accepting that without a trace of skepticism. Another point for him.

"Does that kind of thing happen a lot?"

She shrugged. When you dealt with the public, you were bound to encounter a few entitled assholes. It was just part of the business. That didn't mean she wanted to discuss it.

When she said nothing more, he said, "Those muffins were great."

She fidgeted in her chair and avoided his eyes. Brown with little specks of gold and green, they had a way of making her heart beat a little faster when he looked at her. "Thanks."

"I'm Steve, by the way. I moved into the place next to yours last week."

"I know."

He waited expectantly, and she found herself answering, "I'm Sam."

"Nice to meet you, Sam."

He offered his hand over the table. She looked at it for a moment before taking it. It was huge and rough and warm, and it dwarfed hers.

"I, uh, have to get back to work."

"Okay."

She stood up, and he did, too, collecting his now-empty cup and stuffing the paper napkin and muffin wrappers into it.

"See you around, Sam."

She nodded.

It was only minutes after he left that her heart started slowing to a more acceptable level. He wasn't just good-looking and smacked together; he was also chivalrous and had a shy, almost-awkward charm about him. And when he'd wrapped that big paw around her much smaller hand, she had felt the tingles in the tips of her toes and her nipples. She hadn't expected that.

"Who was that?" Jenna asked, her eyes lit with the same lusty look she had seen other women shooting his way.

"My next-door neighbor," Sam answered.

"Well, damn. Need a roommate?"

Sam didn't answer as she grabbed a few carafes and took them back into the kitchen. Another thing about her new neighbor? She could see herself starting to like him. She was going to have to be very careful from now on.

~ *Anthony* ~

Anthony sat in the corner, seething as he sipped the nonfat mocha Frappuccino—or whatever the college kids were drinking these days—and pretending to be immersed in his book.

He had been so ready to take out the arrogant suit giving Samantha a hard time. He had his hand around the handle of the knife in his pocket, ready to show the pompous ass a thing or two about respect. Then, G.I. Joe had had to step in and ruin everything.

The burn deep in his chest flared as Samantha got up and returned to the counter. G.I. Joe stared at her ass the whole way. Anthony wanted to carve out his eyes for it.

Didn't the thick-necked Neanderthal know that he didn't stand a chance with Samantha? She wasn't foolish enough to fall for some grunting, muscled bootlicker. No, she needed a *smart* man. A man who could think for himself and care for her soul as well as her body.

She needed *him*.

Of course, she didn't know that yet, but she would. Soon. Until then, he would just have to stay vigilant and take care of her from afar until the time was right.

He sat back in his chair, drawing G.I. Joe's gaze. Anthony stared right back.

With his unkempt, long hair tied back in a man bun, thick-rimmed glasses, and Rasta-style hoodie, he looked like one of the students at the local college. There was no way G.I. Joe would recognize him.

No one did, not unless Anthony wanted them to. Not even Samantha. He didn't hold it against her. He was a clever chameleon.

She had felt the pull though. Felt this strange, exciting chemistry they had between them. He could tell by the way she had smiled at him and the way her fingers had lingered just a second longer than necessary when she handed him his change.

He would have to do something about G.I. Joe. He didn't like the way that guy had been sniffing around Samantha. She wasn't interested—that was obvious—but G.I. Joe wasn't taking the hint. If he continued to trespass where he wasn't welcome, Anthony would just have to help him with that.

CHAPTER THREE

~ *Smoke* ~

Smoke tapped the address Church had given him into his GPS and set off. He had meant to get an earlier start, but the coffee shop had been calling him. He could lie to himself and rationalize that he had just been craving a cup of good, strong coffee. Or he could be honest and admit that the particular craving hadn't manifested itself until he caught a glimpse of the logo on his enigmatic new neighbor's shirt, riding the swell of a generous breast.

If he was being honest, he would also have to admit that he would be adding a stop there every morning from now on. Not only was the coffee exceptionally good, but his finely-honed instincts had also told him something was going on with *Sam*, something that had her spooked.

Smoke's lips curled as he recalled how Sam had stood up to that jackoff in the coffee shop. Beneath that skittish rabbit lay a little tigress—he was sure of it. Unfortunately, spirit and courage weren't always enough. Some problems required

physical strength, skill, and a flexible moral
compass.

That was where he came in. He couldn't
explain this sudden, uncharacteristic need to stick
his nose where it didn't belong, but he'd learned to
never ignore his instincts, especially when they
were as strong as this one.

Chances were, his neighbor neither wanted nor
welcomed his interference, and for that reason
alone, he didn't intend for her to know about it. He
would do what he did best—observe from the
shadows and, if necessary, quietly resolve any
threats that arose. Hopefully, it wouldn't come to
that, but his gut told him differently.

One thing he was fairly sure about after that
little exchange he had witnessed earlier: Sam wasn't
the type to be afraid without good reason.

Besides, his conscience wouldn't let him do
anything else. Being a SEAL was as much a part of
who he was as the genetic code he had been born
with. Protecting innocents and eliminating threats
were what he had been trained to do, and he was
damn good at it. Just because he had left active duty
didn't mean he could just turn that shit off. And as
long as he was around, why not? It wasn't like he
had anything better to do. Sitting around, twiddling
his thumbs, wasn't his style.

About twenty minutes out of town, the digital
voice directed him to take the next right off the two-
lane mountain road. Some of the overgrown brush

had been cleared away fairly recently; otherwise, he might have missed the turnoff entirely.

The access road wasn't in great shape. It showed signs of neglect, and years of seasonal freezing and thawing cycles had left cracks and potholes large enough to disable a small car. Smoke was glad for his big tires and sturdy undercarriage, but even in his Jeep, he kept the speed down until he learned the road.

Massive trees reached high on either side, their upper branches leaning toward each other to form a natural arch. Bright green buds and blossoms added to the effect, though the view would look just as good in any season. With each passing minute, he felt more and more like he was leaving the outside world behind and entering another time and place.

When the road finally opened, a breathtaking view was revealed. A hidden valley lay before him, complete with a modest lake and rolling hills. An imposing manor house—what was left of it—sat on top of one of the higher swells, regally overlooking it all.

When Church had told him his plans for turning an old, abandoned resort into a sanctuary for veterans, Smoke had pictured a campground lodge or something. He certainly hadn't imagined anything like *this*.

He continued up to the remains of what had once been the main building, parking his Jeep next to Mad Dog's hulking V8 pickup. The others were already there, milling around.

"Glad you could make it, Smoke." Doc beckoned him to a large folding table, where survey maps sat along with a large pourable carton of coffee, and a couple of boxes of doughnuts from the mini-mart in town.

Smoke poured himself a cup and almost choked on the bitter sludge. That settled it. He was going to stop by Sam's coffeehouse every morning and pick up some real coffee and muffins for these guys. Not only were they far superior, but doing so would also provide another excuse for him to see Sam. A legitimate one at that.

He greeted the guys, most of whom were in high spirits. Clearly, he wasn't the only one feeling the sense of peace around this place. It was good to see. They had all seen enough of the darker side of life. Suddenly, Church's vision seemed a whole lot clearer.

Mad Dog popped an entire doughnut in his mouth and clapped his hands together. "All right, ladies, now that we're all finally here, daylight's burning. Let's get to work."

"Who put you in charge?" Heff grumbled, but his eyes were bright.

"I did," Church said. "He's the only one of us with a degree in architectural engineering."

If the other dropped jaws were any indication, Smoke wasn't the only one who hadn't known that. From what he had been told, Mad Dog was a boss when it came to creating safe holes in practically any environment, but a degree?

"Really?"

Mad Dog nodded, looking somewhat embarrassed as he grabbed another doughnut and loped up to the main building. There was a story there—Smoke was sure of it—but it didn't look like Mad Dog was keen on sharing. That was all right. He would if and when he was ready. Until then, they all had their secrets.

"I'm going to give Smoke the grand tour," Church called out. "Play nice, kids."

A few snorted, but they put down their shitty coffees and followed Mad Dog toward what remained of the manor house.

"This used to be a vacation resort," Church told him as they walked the perimeter of the property. "You wouldn't know it by looking at it now, but it was a really nice place. People would come from miles around to stay here."

There was something raw in Church's voice that made Smoke shoot him a sideways glance. Church was looking ahead, as if picturing the place in his mind.

"You've been here before?"

Church nodded, his face a mask that told Smoke nothing ... and a lot. "Yeah. It was a family-owned thing, passed down from generation to generation. Swimming and boating in the summer, hiking in the fall, skating in the winter—every season had something to offer."

"What happened?"

"A fire," Church said, his voice oddly hollow. "In the middle of the night. There weren't any guests here at the time. The place closed for a couple of weeks every spring for renovations and such. The family though, they were here. They didn't make it."

They continued to walk in silence, Smoke's instincts telling him to remain quiet, that Church wasn't quite done.

"Except the son," Church said finally. "He wasn't here when it happened."

Despite the sun shining down on them, a chill went up and down the length of Smoke's spine. A light breeze blew through the trees, creating a pleasant background for the music of the multitude of birds and woodland creatures who had made this idyllic land their home. Smoke had a pretty good inkling of who that son was.

"You're doing a good thing here, Church."

Church nodded. "*We're* doing a good thing here. Couldn't do it without you guys."

As they made their way around the perimeter and back up to where they had started, Church told Smoke more about his plans. They would concentrate on restoring the main building first, which was where the guests would stay in two- or three-room suites. They would redo the plumbing and electric as well as rebuild the on-site kitchen and put in some common areas. Once that was done, they would expand outward.

Church said he hoped to have at least some parts operational and ready to accept guests by November since the holidays could be a particularly difficult time. Hopefully, being around others who *got it*, who had gone through or were going through the same things, would make it a little easier.

The more Church talked about his plans, the more Smoke realized the guy's passion for his vision, and the more he was on board. There was no doubt a place like this was needed. And with a focused leader like Church at the helm, it was going to be a huge success—of that, he had no doubt.

It would be a daunting task though. The place needed a lot of work—and not just the manor house. The grounds had been neglected too long. Outbuildings—those that weren't piles of rubble—were even worse. The boathouse, dock, stables—they all had to be rebuilt. Add on that Church's dream included private cabins and a state-of-the-art gym/rehab facility, and it seemed impossible.

Good thing they were all SEALs. Pulling off the impossible was what they did.

By the time they rejoined the others, Smoke was feeling pretty stoked about the project. Judging by the way the other guys had rallied, he wasn't the only one. They believed in it, too.

Beyond sharing a common, worthwhile purpose, he felt like he was part of a team again. It felt comfortable, familiar.

Though Church was the official owner of the place, he insisted those of them willing to sign on be partners. He said, if they were going to put in the work to make his vision a reality, then they deserved to reap the benefits as well.

~ *Sam* ~

One of the benefits of starting her workday before dawn was being able to leave before the sun set. Even with the twelve-hour days she typically put in, Sam was able to call it quits around five or so.

The day had gone by quickly. After the morning rush, she had left Jenna in charge out front and gone into the office to handle the business side of things.

The current owner, Mr. Santori, didn't have a head for business. He was a nice man and had the kind of friendly personality that people liked, but his financial sense left a lot to be desired. It was Sam who had brought the old place out of financial ruin. If things continued as they were, next quarter might just see them back in the black.

She called distributors, scheduled deliveries, and generally made sure things ran smoothly. It was a lot of work, but the shop was going to be hers soon, so it was worth it.

The moment she stepped out of the café and back into the real world, the usual uneasiness returned with a vengeance. Inside the shop, her mind and body were constantly busy, and people were always around. Once outside, she was alone again, and the fear began to take hold.

Sam shook it off, chastising herself for being a paranoid fraidy-cat. She was a grown woman, one who had been living on her own and taking care of herself for years. This feeling of vulnerability wasn't her, and she didn't like it one bit.

So her previous place had been broken into. Big deal. Lots of people had their homes burglarized. It probably wasn't personal, just someone out to steal something and turn it into a quick buck.

But then why hadn't it felt that way? Why was her place the only one targeted? Why hadn't anything of value been stolen? She wasn't even sure anything *had* been taken. A few articles of clothing were missing, but she might have lost those at the Laundromat.

And months later, why did she still feel the need to look over her shoulder constantly?

She'd asked herself these questions a hundred times over, and she kept coming back to the same answer—it *was* personal, and it was about more than a simple snatch and grab. That was the only answer that made sense despite what the police had said.

Sam pushed those thoughts to the back of her mind as she visited the grocery store around the block. She picked up a few things for dinner, then went to the post office to check the box where she had forwarded all her mail. There was very little there. A fundraising letter from her university alumni association, a local coupon publication, and an offer for a great deal on a home equity loan.

With her cash running low, she had planned on hitting the ATM on the way back, too, but that uncomfortable feeling of being watched continued to grow. She bypassed the bank and quickened her steps, intent on making it back to her apartment building before dark.

By the time she arrived, her heart was racing, and she was breathing heavily. Her hands were shaking as she tried to jam her key into the outside door.

"Hey, Sam."

Sam shrieked, swirling around at the same time she took a step back. Keys in one hand, her reusable grocery bag hanging from her arm, her finger poised above the plunger on a can of pepper spray, she looked up into the concerned eyes of her new neighbor.

"Everything okay?" he asked, eyeing her skeptically.

"Yeah. You startled me!" Heat rose in her cheeks and she averted her eyes, feeling ten kinds of foolish. "You shouldn't sneak up on people like that."

"I'm sorry. I didn't realize I was sneaking."

"Well, you were."

Aware of his body heat licking along her back and the scent of clean male sweat, she managed to unlock the door, unable to cross the threshold into the lobby fast enough.

She went over to the elevator and jabbed the button. The doors opened immediately, and she stepped inside the car. Though she preferred to ride alone, she figured it would be terribly rude if she didn't hold the doors open. It wasn't as if she could pretend she hadn't seen him there.

When he didn't follow in behind her, she peeked her head out to find him still standing by the door, watching.

"Coming?" she asked.

He shook his head. "No, thanks. I'll take the stairs. I'm not fit for sharing an enclosed space right now."

Before the doors closed, Sam registered his appearance in the bright lights of the foyer, overriding her inexplicable fear. His hair was mussed, and streaks of dirt and sawdust stuck to his faded jeans and classic men's cotton tee, clinging tightly to his muscled body. The work boots covering his exceptionally large feet were well-worn and dirty. The man looked and smelled good, even when he was hot and sweaty. How was that fair?

The moment the doors opened again on the seventh floor, Sam made a beeline for her apartment.

"Samantha, is everything all right? You look pale, dear."

Sam closed her eyes briefly and pasted on a smile before turning to the old woman who lived across the hall. Trying to avoid her had become a daily challenge.

It wasn't that Sam didn't like her elderly neighbor; it was just that Sam wasn't really into the gossipy type of chitchat at which Mrs. Himmelwright excelled. She had actually seen the woman open her door and dust the peephole several times when the apartment next to hers was being shown to prospective renters.

Perhaps a subtle hint would work.

"I'm fine, Mrs. Himmelwright. Just tired. It's been a long day."

"Have you met our new neighbor?"

So much for that. She should have known Mrs. Himmelwright would ask about Steve, anxious for information. He was new, good-looking, and presumably single, which officially made him prime fodder for speculative scuttlebutt.

"Yes," she said simply.

Sam looked toward the stairwell, where, at any second, the man himself would be appearing in all his sexy, dirty, sweaty glory. She had been hoping to get inside her place before that happened.

"And …"

Sam exhaled, then pushed her key into the lock. "And nothing."

"Hmpf." Mrs. Himmelwright sniffed, clearly unhappy with Sam's answer. "Well, if he throws any wild parties, I'm calling the building manager."

"You do that, Mrs. Himmelwright. Have a good night."

Sam turned the key and opened her door, slipping inside before her elderly neighbor could say any more on the subject. She engaged the locks, then waited by the door. In some ways, she supposed that made her no better than Mrs. Himmelwright.

Within seconds, she heard the stairwell door open and close. She looked through her peephole, seeing Mrs. Himmelwright still standing in her open doorway, not even trying to hide her interest. Steve nodded to the old woman politely.

While he was at his door, Sam distinctly heard him say quietly, "Have a good night, Sam."

"You, too, Steve," she murmured.

She could have sworn she saw his lips quirk into a tired smile.

As had become habit, Sam worked her way around her apartment, turning on the lights and checking to see that everything was exactly the way she had left it. Convinced that all was in order, she turned off every light but the one in her kitchenette and opened windows to let in the fresh, cool air of the evening.

While she prepared a quick dinner, she gave herself another mental pep talk. Rather than getting better with time, her anxiety seemed to be worsening. Other than the sensation of being watched, nothing had happened for a while now. That was something, wasn't it? Maybe whoever had been stalking her had finally moved on.

The police didn't seem to think the break-in six months ago was related to the other weird things that had been happening, like the flowers that had been anonymously delivered to the coffee shop or the occasional cards left at her mailbox. Even if there *was* a connection, they had told her no laws had been broken and no threats had been made. It wasn't illegal to send someone flowers or leave a pleasant note.

Even if it was incredibly creepy.

Visions of her new neighbor snuck into her thoughts later that evening as she soaked in her tub, then climbed into bed. He seemed like a nice enough guy. Handsome. Gentlemanly. Tall, broad, and strong with a simmering undercurrent of danger about him.

She could even see herself being attracted to him. She wasn't about to start anything though. She had goals, and once Mr. Santori signed the coffee shop over to her, she would be too busy to invest time in a relationship. But, she thought as she turned off the light and snuggled between the sheets, having someone like him next door made her feel a little safer. Perhaps, if and when she saw him again, she would try to be a bit more neighborly.

~ *Anthony* ~

Hidden among the foliage of the trees, Anthony exhaled slowly as he saw Samantha's light go out. Then, he adjusted his nightscope slightly to the left.

G.I. Joe was on his balcony, drinking a beer in the dark. The cocky bastard didn't realize just how vulnerable he was. Didn't know how easily Anthony could pick him off. No one would be the wiser. One shot, right between the eyes, was all it would take.

As satisfying as that thought was, it would raise too many questions and draw too much attention. The guy deserved to die—no doubt about it—but later, when Anthony and Samantha were ready to embark on their new life together.

What was the guy's plan anyway? To come off all badass in an attempt to impress her? Did he really believe beautiful, intelligent women like Samantha responded to those kinds of caveman tactics?

Well, even if some did, *she* didn't. Anthony had seen her rebuff the advances of the many men who tried to flirt with her. She was too classy to fall for strapping muscles or expensive suits. She looked deeper than the surface. That made her better than all of them.

That guy though, he wasn't going to simply take no for an answer. No, Anthony had seen the blatant interest in his eyes. Sam's new neighbor looked at her like he was a predator and she was his prey.

Well, who's the prey now, pretty boy?

As if G.I. Joe had heard his thoughts, the guy on the balcony turned his head and glared right at him.

Anthony froze and held his breath. There was no way the guy could see him. It was dark, and he was too well hidden in the trees. He remained motionless anyway.

Eventually, the guy went back inside. Anthony wasted no time in putting away his scope and sliding off into the darkness with but one thought—*G.I. Joe has to go.*

CHAPTER FOUR

~ *Smoke* ~

Smoke was already halfway down the block, tucked invisibly between buildings, when Sam emerged the next morning. Using the skills for which he had been nicknamed, he stayed in the shadows while following her progress.

When she first passed by where he was hidden, she hesitated slightly, as if sensing his presence, then quickened her pace. Smoke smiled grimly to himself. The woman had good instincts, and that only reinforced his questionable decision to play silent bodyguard.

He tried to tell himself that he would be compelled to do the same for anyone, but that wasn't true. For some reason he couldn't quite fathom, his neighbor was *different*. He couldn't stop thinking about her.

It wasn't as if she had been trying to get his attention. Just the opposite in fact. She didn't seem interested in him at all. Maybe that had something to do with it. Women, even those who had no intention of engaging, often flirted with him or looked at him a certain way. Just because he wasn't interested didn't mean he wasn't aware.

That wasn't an overinflated ego talking. He wasn't special. Every man on his team got the same treatment. Just as most men couldn't help noticing a beautiful, curvaceous woman, most women responded to a cut physique and the quiet confidence that said a man knew he was the biggest, baddest thing in the room.

But not his neighbor.

Oh, there had been a brief flare of feminine appreciation in her pretty gray-green eyes, but she hadn't seemed inclined to acknowledge it. That, along with the sense that she was in danger, intrigued him. Besides, if he concentrated on her and her problems, he wouldn't have to think about his own.

Once he was sure she was safely in the coffee shop, he looped around and headed toward the park. It took only minutes to find what he had been looking for—the depressions between trunks of thick evergreens that suggested someone had been standing there for some time.

He peered through the branches, confirming his earlier suspicions. Not only had he felt sights on him after Sam's light went out the night before, but he had seen the telltale flash of something metallic. A watch maybe or a ring.

Whoever the unwelcome observer was, he had left no further evidence of his presence. The watcher was a novice, but a novice with enough skill to be dangerous.

Smoke returned to his apartment, his mind working, assembling the pieces. Who was stalking his neighbor, and why? Was he dangerous or just a harmless Peeping Tom?

Smoke made a mental note to talk to Cage. According to Church, Cage was the go-to guy when it came to needing intel. Maybe he could provide some information and fill in a few blanks, starting with Sam's full name.

After changing into manual labor–appropriate clothing, Smoke stopped by the café, pleased to find another line. It would give him time to observe.

A few college kids huddled over a round table in the corner, looking at something on an iPad. An elderly man sipped his coffee, his eyes flicking between the stack of papers in front of him and an older woman two tables over.

The back of Smoke's neck prickled, but not in a bad way, drawing his attention over to the other side of the café, where a pair of attractive women in business casual were giving him appreciative glances.

He didn't acknowledge them one way or the other. He wasn't here for them. The pretty brunette he *was* here for was too busy to notice him as he slowly advanced toward the front counter.

Nothing out of the ordinary happened. There were no pricks in the line ahead of him, and that sense of danger he had felt yesterday was noticeably absent today.

"Six extra-large coffees and a dozen muffins, please."

Her eyes widened when she realized he was the next customer, but then her pretty pink lips quirked when he gave his order. "Feeling especially hungry and thirsty this morning, Steve?"

He grinned back, ignoring the way his balls suddenly tightened at the sound of his name on her lips. "Yes, but those aren't all for me."

"Sure they're not. Whatever you say." Her eyes twinkled, and, damn, he liked that, too.

What was this? Were they flirting? Suddenly, he felt awkward. Normal, everyday things like playful banter weren't on his radar. Then, she smiled at him again, and he didn't care.

She put the coffees in a convenient carry tray, then filled a to-go box with an assortment of muffins that made his mouth water. "Try not to eat them all at once," she teased.

"I will, but no promises. These things are addictive. My compliments to the chef."

A light flush rose in her cheeks, but he could tell she was pleased.

Satisfied she was safe for now, he paid for his purchases. "Thanks, Sam. See you tomorrow."

~ Sam ~

So, he's planning on coming back, is he? The thought shouldn't have been as appealing as it was.

Sam watched her neighbor walk out of the coffee shop, balancing the tray of coffees and box of muffins in those mitt-sized hands of his. Visions of exactly what he could do with those hands commandeered her thoughts for a moment until the next customer's deliberate throat clearing brought her back to the present.

"Yeah, I'd hit that."

Sam's gaze snapped to the thirty-something whose eyes were glued to the back pockets of Steve's snug-fitting jeans. Only once he had disappeared out the door did the woman look back at Sam.

"Friend of yours?"

"Neighbor," Sam answered truthfully.

"Lucky you."

The surprising and totally irrational ripple of jealousy faded at the customer's words, even as the also surprising and irrational words, *Yes, I am*, almost shot out of her mouth. Simply knowing she would be seeing more of Steve and this put-together woman wouldn't was oddly satisfying.

Also satisfying, Mr. Santori was looking over the quarterly reports she had put together in preparation for his upcoming meeting with his lawyer. They showed a marked improvement in the business, thanks to her hard work. Her business degree and years of working in her grandparents' bakery were paying off. She was finally going to get a place of her own!

That afternoon, Sam left the café, feeling optimistic, but the feeling didn't last. That warning prickle, the one that made her feel as if she was being watched, started up again when she was about to leave the ATM. As she waited for her receipt to print, she tried to remain calm and casual as she looked around. That was when she noticed Steve coming out of the bank.

Without hesitation, she ripped the receipt from the slot and walked toward him with quick, deliberate steps, intending to intercept. He looked much as he had the day before, as if he had just come from working outside. She couldn't help wondering what he did. Whatever it was, it wasn't spending his days sitting passively behind a desk somewhere.

His firm male lips turned up when he spotted her, sending a pleasant, tingling sensation into her belly and below.

"We've got to stop meeting like this," he quipped.

Something like relief settled over her, allowing a nervous chuckle to escape. "Our paths do seem to be crossing quite often," she agreed.

"Must be fate," he said with the hint of a smile. "Are you heading back to your apartment?"

She nodded.

"Me, too. Mind if I walk with you?"

"Not at all," she said maybe a little too quickly, if the way his eyes narrowed was any indication.

Thankfully, he didn't call her on it.

"I think I might have unknowingly created a few monsters today," he said casually as they walked along.

His legs were much longer than hers, but he slowed his pace for her. She appreciated that.

"Oh? And why is that?"

"The guys loved the coffee and muffins. They're demanding I bring them every day now."

She laughed softly. "I'm glad. If you're serious, I can have something ready for you. That way, you won't have to wait as long."

"Oh, I'm serious. They threatened to go on strike if I don't."

"Well, we can't have that."

"Definitely not."

They walked the rest of the way in a comfortable, companionable silence. As he had the night before, he hung back near the stairwell when she went for the elevator.

"Trust me," she said, holding the doors open, "you're fine."

He grinned, sending more sparks shooting into areas that hadn't experienced sparks for a long time.

"If you're sure."

"I'm sure."

After another moment or two of hesitation, he joined her in the elevator car. Though he didn't crowd her, his presence did manage to fill the space around her. She was acutely aware of his scent— woodsy with a touch of sawdust and very masculine. Hardly off-putting. On the contrary, it conjured images of sultry nights and naked bodies.

"Hey, uh, Sam," he said almost shyly as they reached their floor.

"Yes?" Heat flooded her cheeks. Surely, he hadn't read her mind.

"Do you know any good takeout places that deliver around here? I haven't had a chance to pick up much in the way of food and cooking supplies yet."

She paused, somewhat relieved and disappointed that he hadn't asked her something else.

"What do you like?"

"I'm a guy. I like meat." He laughed. "But I'm not really into fast food."

"Hmm … well, there's really not a lot of options unless you're willing to drive out to Pine Ridge. Sumneyville only has one restaurant," she told him. "Franco's doesn't deliver, but they do call-aheads and curbside pickup."

"That works for me. I can order something for both of us, pick it up, and bring it back here."

Sam hesitated at the door, the desire to say yes surprisingly strong. However, something held her back.

Was he asking her out? Or just being neighborly? It was impossible to tell by his hooded expression.

She forced the words out before she started something she might regret. "No, but thanks."

Disappointment flashed briefly in his eyes. "Okay then. Have a good evening."

"Thanks. You, too."

Sam stepped into her apartment, hearing his door close a moment later. She exhaled heavily. Had she just made a mistake by refusing his offer? She was tired, and she really didn't feel like cooking for herself, yet she hadn't wanted to give him the wrong impression either. Yeah, he was extremely good-looking and sparked an interest she hadn't felt in a long time, but she wasn't exactly in a good place to start anything. Plus, purely physical relationships weren't her thing, no matter how much her body might be disagreeing with her at that moment.

As was her routine, she turned on her lights and opened the windows, checked the closets and made use of the bathroom. Everything seemed okay.

She had only taken a few steps into her bedroom when the heavy scent hit her. She froze, her gaze landing on the bouquet of colorful flowers on her dresser.

Then, she screamed.

~ *Anthony* ~

Anthony watched from the corner bus stop as Samantha and that tenacious meathead walked down the street together. They didn't appear to be talking to one another. Samantha kept her gaze ahead while her irritating companion discreetly scanned the surrounding area.

Anthony held his breath as G.I. Joe's gaze briefly landed on him, then let it out as it swiveled elsewhere.

Did he know?

No, he couldn't possibly know. Anthony had been too careful. He had covered his tracks well. By the time G.I. Joe figured it out—*if* he ever did—he and Samantha would be long gone.

Nevertheless, until then, the guy would remain an irritant. He was clearly interested in Samantha— another dog after Anthony's girl.

He didn't blame Samantha though. She couldn't help that she was beautiful and that other men were naturally attracted to her.

Anthony didn't like other men looking at her like that. If she had scars, like him, they would leave her alone. Not him though. Unlike those mangy curs who just wanted her for her pretty face and curvy body, Anthony loved her for what she was on the inside.

That was why he had left her the flowers—so

she would know.

He had left something for G.I. Joe, too. He hoped they both enjoyed their surprises.

CHAPTER FIVE

~ *Smoke* ~

"Way to go, dumbass," Smoke muttered to himself.

For a few moments there, he had thought she might be receptive to extending their time together. Her quick refusal had been both polite and very clear, proving that, once again, he was incapable of reading signals.

He could have sworn she was glad to see him when he showed up outside the ATM and that she had appreciated the company. Add in the subtle teasing banter from earlier and her invitation to join him in the elevator, and he had thought maybe …

Ah, well. It was best not to complicate things. He could—and would—continue to look out for her, at least while he was around.

The moment Smoke stepped over the threshold, his senses rocketed to high alert. He drew the concealed weapon he always carried and listened intently, his eyes making a careful sweep. In the silence, he could just barely hear Sam moving around her place, performing what he now recognized as a regular after-work ritual on her part.

Nothing looked out of place, but something felt wrong. He moved swiftly and quietly throughout the apartment. Without much in the way of furniture and minimal draperies, there weren't many places an intruder could hide. Someone had been in here though. He would bet his Budweiser—his SEAL trident pin—on it.

He paused at the closed bathroom door. A shushing sound, very faint, came from within. Inhaling slowly and gun in hand, he eased the door open and reached for the switch.

As the bathroom flooded with light, the coiled pit viper in the tub lunged up in a strike.

"Fucking hell!" Smoke muttered, shutting the door immediately.

Having grown up along a river in the northeastern US, he had recognized it immediately for what it was—a copperhead. The species was venomous, but not usually lethal. That didn't mean their bites weren't damn painful and something to be avoided.

He went into his bedroom and grabbed a pillow, peeling off the case. If at all possible, he would capture the thing and dispose of it elsewhere.

Then, he heard Sam scream.

Leaving the snake to deal with later, Smoke rushed out of his place and banged on Sam's locked door, hoping to hell she hadn't found a similar surprise in her bathroom.

"Sam! Open up! It's Steve."

He didn't have to knock again. Seconds later, Sam opened the door, her face pale and her eyes fearful. He held her gently by the upper arms, scanning her for bite marks or injuries.

"Are you all right? What happened?"

She shook her head. "I'm not hurt," she said, her voice shaky. "But someone's been in my apartment."

"What makes you say that?" he asked carefully.

"Because whoever it was, they left me flowers in my bedroom."

Well, that was creepy as hell, but it was definitely better than a copperhead in the bathroom.

"Have you noticed anything else? Any more surprises? Anything missing?"

"No, I don't think so. I usually walk through the place when I come home. The bedroom is the last place I check."

"Mind if I have a look around?"

She shook her head again, stepping back and wrapping her arms around herself.

Smoke did a quick yet thorough inspection, paying particular attention to the bathroom, but he didn't find anything out of the ordinary.

When he returned to the living room, Sam was still standing by the door, right where he had left her. Huge eyes, the color of a perfect stormy sky, looked up at him. Deep inside his chest, something clenched. The muscles in his arms bunched and flexed with the desire to pull her close and erase the fear he saw there.

He might have been tempted to do it, too, if he hadn't recalled just how easily she had shut him down just a short while earlier. The word *KISS* popped into his mind—Keep It Simple, Stupid. Yet the acronym conjured up something else entirely when Sam was looking up at him like that. He had to rein those errant urges in before he screwed up again.

"Everything looks okay, but we should call the police."

She nodded. "I will, but I don't know what good it will do."

The way she had said it made him think this wasn't the first time something like this had happened. With any luck, Cage would be able to provide some insight. Smoke had asked him to do some research while they were working up at the resort earlier, and though he had gotten a raised eyebrow at the request, Cage had agreed without asking a lot of questions.

Hopefully, Sam would provide some firsthand info, but he wanted to calm her down first. That fearful look in her eyes made him want to kill the bastard who had put it there.

"Come on; you can call from my place."

She opened her mouth, as if to argue, but closed it again. "All right. Let me just grab my purse. It has my phone and wallet."

She followed him back to his apartment, which looked stark and utilitarian compared to the soft hues and homey feel of hers.

He waved his hand toward the recliner. "Sorry, this is all the seating space I have at the moment. Make your call. I'm going to grab a quick shower."

Remembering his own little *welcome home* surprise, he disappeared into his bedroom first and picked up the pillowcase and a change of clothes.

His gut told him that whoever had left the flowers in Sam's bedroom was also the one who had left the copperhead for him. He had seen enough to believe someone was stalking her. It wasn't a stretch to assume said stalker had been watching and seen them together. The snake was probably meant as a warning—a special *stay away from Sam* message.

If that were true, then the guy wasn't nearly as smart as he thought he was. If anything, his latest actions only made Smoke more determined to stay close and keep an eye on things.

After brief consideration, he decided against telling Sam that he had received a "gift," too. It would only upset her more and could be counterproductive. She seemed like the kind of person who would distance herself if she felt like she was putting someone else in danger—even if that someone was a lethal, highly skilled SEAL—and that was unacceptable.

As far as telling the cops, he would play it by

ear, see how they responded. He preferred to handle things his own way if possible. Police had rules to follow, laws to uphold. Him, not so much. For the last twelve years, his primary objectives had taken precedence over things like red tape and working through proper channels. Those restrictions could take months, even years, and he had neither the patience nor the time for that. He wanted to know that, when he moved on, Sam would be safe.

With that in mind, Smoke made quick work of the snake, dispatching it as humanely as possible and tying it up in the case. He could hear Sam's muffled voice through the doorway, talking to the police. He took a two-minute shower to get off the worst of the day's dirt and sweat, then changed and was back in the living room five minutes later.

"That was fast," she said. Her eyes latched on to the water droplets that fell from his still-wet hair down onto his shoulder and unconsciously licked her lips.

Another signal to misinterpret? He put a lock on the poorly timed and wholly inappropriate lust flaring up from the base of his spine.

Her eyes flicked back up to his face. He needed to focus on something other than how that little pink tongue would feel on his skin.

"I'm guessing you were in the military," she said.

He nodded but didn't offer any additional information, and she didn't ask.

"The police said they'll send someone out when they can, but it might be a few hours. I'm not supposed to touch anything until then."

"Standard procedure," Smoke commented. "You can hang out with me." The words were spoken for her benefit. He had no intention of letting her out of his sight.

She chewed her lip, then raised her eyes to his. "I think I'd like that, if you're sure you don't mind."

"Not at all. I'll even let you ride in my Jeep when we go for food." He wasn't asking this time, and this wasn't a date. It was simply a way to feed his need for food while satisfying this other need to stay with her until the police arrived.

Again, she looked like she wanted to say something but wisely refrained.

He pulled up the restaurant's menu on his phone, then dialed, turning to Sam while he was put on hold. "You like steak?"

"Yes, but you don't have to—"

"Two New York strip dinners, baked potatoes, garden salad." He spoke into the phone, overriding her protest. "House is fine, on the side. Carry-out. Got it."

"You didn't need to do that," she said as soon as he hung up.

He shrugged. "You have to eat, don't you? Besides, good manners dictate that I can't eat unless you're eating, and I'm starving."

Her lips quirked at that, easing some of the

tension around that pretty mouth. "What if I'm not hungry?"

"Trust me, it won't go to waste," he said, grabbing his keys. "Let's go. We want to be here when the cops show. Uh, wait a sec."

Smoke went into the bathroom, grabbed the knotted-up pillowcase with the dead snake inside, then held open the door for her.

"What's that?" she asked, looking suspiciously at his bundle.

"Garbage."

"In a pillowcase?"

"I haven't had time to get garbage bags yet."

Her eyes widened slightly, and then she laughed. It was a light, beautiful sound.

"You really need to get to the store, Steve."

He grinned back. "Yeah, I guess I should, huh?"

~ *Sam* ~

Sam laughed, then felt foolish. Once again, her living space had been violated by some unknown creeper, yet here she was, laughing at something her neighbor had said. Her handsome, sexy, kind, chivalrous neighbor.

His smile faded along with hers, and then he reached down and wrapped his massive hand around hers. "It's okay, Sam," he said gently.

"*You're* okay. We'll get this sorted out, all right?"

She nodded. Somehow, she could almost believe him.

With a brief stop at the dumpster, he led her to his Jeep. It was a rugged-looking thing, exactly the type of vehicle a man like him should drive. He teased her about her petite stature when he put both of those big paws around her waist and lifted her up into the seat, but she barely noticed. She was too focused on the lingering heat where his hands had been.

The ride to and from the restaurant was uneventful but informative. For instance, she learned that Steve was adept at driving stick shift, kept his vehicle as clean as he did his apartment, and had a thing for hard rock music.

They ate together on his living room floor, picnic-style, sitting upon a blanket he had pulled out of the back of his Jeep and using the plastic utensils provided with the takeout. Sam hadn't thought she would be able to eat much, but the food was delicious and the company pleasant. Steve didn't pry or ask a lot of personal questions, and for that alone, she was grateful.

They kept the conversation light. Sam told him she had spent most of her life in the area and provided a bit of local history. Being with him was easy once she managed to get over her initial anxiety. When the police arrived nearly three hours later, she was shocked to see just how much time had passed.

Far calmer than she had been earlier, Sam let the officers into her apartment and explained what had happened. Steve was a constant, calming presence, except when one of the officers muttered an insensitive remark about most women being happy to get flowers.

Steve stiffened and told him, "Most women are not happy about having their apartments broken into."

The chastised officer apologized immediately, and she shot Steve an appreciative glance. It wasn't often that someone stood up for her, and that was twice in as many days that he had done so.

The officers looked around but, unsurprisingly, found nothing useful. Just like last time, the trespasser had left no clues, no hint of his identity or what connection he had to her.

Since nothing had been taken and there were no signs of forced entry, there wasn't anything they could do, except suggest she get the locks changed.

Steve didn't look any happier with their lack of action than she was, but having been through it before, it was nothing less than she had expected.

"I don't think you should stay here, Sam, not till you can get the locks changed."

She sighed. "I don't think I can stay here at all even if I do get the locks changed. The same thing happened in my previous apartment, and I couldn't sleep a wink afterward."

His brows pulled together. "This has happened before?"

"Yes. About six months ago. I ended up staying in a motel until this apartment opened up."

"That settles it then. You can crash at my place till we get this figured out."

"What? No! I can't do that!"

"Why not?" He shrugged.

"I don't even know you."

He frowned. "No, I guess you don't. And my word isn't good enough."

"I didn't mean it that way."

"I know. But you're right. You don't know me. Go with your instincts, Sam. Always."

That was part of the problem. Her instincts wanted her to attach herself to his strong, capable self and be sheltered from this insanity, if only for a little while. Her wallet agreed. Even a cheap motel would cut into her savings, and she was trying to save up as much as she could for a down payment on the café. It was her head that was mucking up the works, but even that was waffling.

She straightened her shoulders and took a deep breath, not quite believing what she was about to say. "You're right; I should go by my instincts, and right now, they're telling me the safest place for me is with you."

~ Anthony ~

Anthony tucked his hands into his pockets and watched with a handful of curious onlookers who had gathered across the street, wondering what had brought the cops out. Inside, he smiled at the thought of the present he had left for G.I. Joe. Oh, how he wished he could have seen the expression on his face! Even better, maybe the snake had bitten him, and he had made a 911 call.

Pussy.

His inner smile turned to a frown, however, when he saw one of the uniforms carry a vase of flowers out of the building and put it into the cruiser. The flowers that *he* had placed in Samantha's bedroom.

Hadn't she liked them? Didn't she know how much they had cost? And what had happened with the snake? He'd spent hours in the mountains, trying to capture one.

He turned away, frustrated. Things were *not* going according to plan.

If wooing Samantha with flowers and love notes wasn't working, he'd have to take things to the next level.

CHAPTER SIX

~ *Smoke* ~

"Not a chance." Smoke crossed his arms over his chest and glared at his obstinate little neighbor. He had to admit, she looked damn cute, curled up on his recliner like that, but it was a no-go.

"I'm *not* taking your bed," she said adamantly.

He growled softly in the back of his throat.

Instead of being swayed, she *smiled* at him. "Does that actually work? The growling thing?"

"Yes," he answered honestly, but things didn't typically reach this stage. The menacing glare and stance were usually enough to get people to see his side of things.

"Well, it won't work with me. If I can't sleep in your recliner, then I'm going to a motel."

"Stubborn female," he muttered.

"Welcome to Sam 101." She smirked, a triumphant gleam in her eye, knowing she had him. "I appreciate the offer—I really do—but I just can't. I already feel like I'm taking advantage of you."

He snorted. Clearly, they had different ideas as to what constituted "taking advantage" of someone.

His idea involved his bed, too, but in his version, she was naked and screaming his name in ecstasy.

He shook his head to dispel the images that had been assaulting his brain since she had gone back to her place to change into appropriate sleepwear and returned, wearing loose-fitting sweats and a modest tank. There was nothing remotely sexy about the outfit, yet he had been sporting a persistent hard-on ever since. She hadn't even taken her bra off, for fuck's sake. That hadn't stopped him from noticing the way her nipples hardened to tight peaks when he walked out of his bedroom without a shirt on.

That might have been a *slightly* intentional move on his part. As a SEAL, he had been trained to use whatever means were at his disposal. Having her focused on his chest was a hell of a lot better than having her think about what had put her in his apartment in the first place. And knowing that he wasn't the only one experiencing a physical attraction made him feel better.

"Well, *Steve 101* stresses the importance of making sure neighbors in distress are as comfortable as possible."

Her lips parted slightly, and then her eyes softened. "Then, you've succeeded. I *am* comfortable here, really. If I took your bed, I wouldn't be able to sleep a wink."

Neither would he, but for totally different reasons.

He exhaled heavily. "All right. You win … this

time."

Her smile was brilliant. "Thank you, Steve. Good night."

"Good night, Sam. Sleep well."

With gnawing reluctance, he left her there, curled up in his recliner like a little kitten, and went into his bedroom, leaving the door slightly ajar so he would hear her if she got up.

And hear her, he did.

Just after midnight, her soft moans brought him back out to investigate. A swath of silvery moonlight revealed Sam in the grips of an erotic dream. He watched, transfixed, until she breathed his name on a soft cry. Her features relaxed, and then she snuggled back into the blankets with a smile on her face.

He groaned inwardly. His dick was now painfully hard, and she was officially under his skin.

Hours later, he still couldn't get the image of Sam's sleep climax out of his mind. He had even resorted to some soapy shower DIY to take the edge off. Didn't last long though. All she had to do was smile at him that morning, and, *bam*, he was right back where he had started.

Clearly, he had gone far too long without the pleasure of a woman's company, but apparently, his long-absent ability to be interested in a woman had returned with a vengeance. Even the cool, crisp mountain air couldn't completely dispel her subtle, lingering vanilla-and-honey scent.

"Did you get the information I asked for?" Smoke asked, handing Cage his coffee.

Cage nodded. "Are you going to tell me what your sudden interest is in Samantha Appelhoff?"

"She's in the apartment next to mine."

"So?"

"So, she's nice."

"She's nice," Cage parroted.

"Yeah, she's nice," he said maybe a bit too defensively, if Cage's smirk was any indication.

"I'm sure you've met a lot of 'nice' girls, Smoke. Are you in the habit of cyberstalking all of them?"

"It's not cyberstalking," Smoke muttered irritably. "I think she's in some kind of trouble."

Cage's expression sobered. "What kind of trouble?"

"She's scared. I think someone's been stalking her for real. There was a bouquet of flowers waiting for her in her apartment when she got home from work yesterday. Her *locked* apartment. They were probably from the same guy who left a copperhead in my bathtub."

"What the fuck?"

Smoke nodded grimly. "That's what I'm trying to figure out. What did you come up with?"

"Well, I think you might be right about the stalking. She's filed several police reports over the last couple of years, claiming someone keeps sending her flowers and leaving her notes and that someone entered her previous residence and went through her things."

"Anything come of it?"

"No." Cage shook his head. "Plying someone with gifts isn't illegal. There was no sign of forced entry with the break-in. Whoever it was, he wasn't kind enough to leave any useful evidence behind."

"Same MO then," Smoke commented.

"I could tap into the building's security camera files, maybe check out some local CCTV video, and see what's up."

"Do it," Smoke told him. "The parking lot, too."

Smoke hadn't forgotten the weird vibes and odd behavior of the guy in the sedan. Maybe the video would provide a clearer picture—if not of his face, then of his license plate.

"Hey, Smoke, how personal is this?"

"Why do you ask?"

Cage shrugged, grabbing a muffin. "Because it's nice to see you give a shit about something."

Cage walked away, leaving Smoke feeling stunned. Had it been that obvious?

Maybe it had.

Since officially leaving the SEALs, he'd been at a loss. He didn't regret his decision; he'd known deep down that it was time. However, he hadn't expected the sense of emptiness that came with it. He'd always had a purpose, a goal to work for, and then suddenly … nothing. That was why he'd finally given in and accepted Church's offer—and why a place like this was so important.

He finished his coffee, then grabbed a sledgehammer and a wheelbarrow and went to work.

~ *Sam* ~

Sam wiped down tables, then refilled the dispensers while she waited for Steve. He'd walked her to work that morning and kept her company until she took the first batches of muffins out of the oven. He also asked that she wait for him to walk her home. Since he'd asked *nicely* and not ordered, as seemed to be his way, she had agreed.

She worried about taking advantage of his kindness, but refusing to take any money for the coffee and muffins eased her conscience somewhat.

Steve had told her that he and some of his friends were working on building a place specifically for vets returning from service. Even if she hadn't felt indebted to Steve for his kindness, she would have insisted on giving him the stuff on the house, gladly paying for it out of her own pocket for such a worthwhile cause.

Mr. Santori came through the front door, surprised to see her still there.

"How did the meeting with the lawyer go?" she asked eagerly.

The older man had left around noon to meet with his lawyer to start the legal paperwork on the transfer of ownership. Only a year earlier, Mr. Santori had been on the verge of declaring bankruptcy and losing the place to a bank auction. She convinced him to sell to her instead, *if* she could turn the place around. Well, she had done that and more. Now, Mr. Santori could retire with a nice nest egg, and she could finally realize her dream of having her own place.

"It went well," he said. He played with the brim of his hat—he always wore a hat outside—and shifted his weight, avoiding her eyes. "What are you still doing here?"

"I always work till at least five," she told him.

Since he spent most of his afternoons down the street at the local VFW, he probably didn't know that. Judging by the flush of his cheeks, he had headed there after the lawyer's office.

"Ah, of course. Well, looks like it's time for you to go then."

Something about his behavior was off. Normally smiling and pleasant, he seemed uncharacteristically uncomfortable.

"Mr. Santori, what's going on?"

"Nothing's going on. I don't want to keep you. Don't you have to get home?"

Now, she *knew* something was fishy. If his anxious behavior hadn't tipped her off, the way he refused to look her in the eye while practically pushing her out the door would have.

"Not immediately, no. What happened at the lawyer's office that you're not telling me?"

He exhaled heavily and pointed to a table. "Sit down, Sam."

She did, dread pooling in her stomach. Nothing good ever came out of a conversation that began with averted gazes and the words, *Sit down, Sam.*

Sit down, Sam. Someone from Health and Family Services needs to talk with you.

Sit down, Sam. You didn't get the scholarship.

Sit down, Sam. There was a fire, and your grandparents were asleep ...

"The thing is, Sam, you've done a tremendous job, turning this place around. Business is better than it's ever been."

She nodded in acknowledgment. He wasn't telling her anything she didn't already know. She had been busting her hump for months, trying to fix the place up and untangle the financial mess he had made.

"And, well, I took those financial reports you had done to my lawyer, and he said I can get a lot more for the place now. He advised me to put it on the market at a higher price."

She gaped at him, certain she had heard wrong. "What? We had an agreement, Mr. Santori! If I proved I could handle the business, you promised to sell it to me. You know I can't afford any more than what we agreed upon."

"I know, Sam, and I'm sorry about that. My lawyer said since there's nothing in writing, what we talked about isn't legally binding, and I need to think about my retirement."

"Your *retirement*?" she said, struggling for control. "You wouldn't have *anything* if you'd been forced to declare bankruptcy."

He stiffened. "Now, Sam, let's not get nasty. It's nothing personal, just business."

"That's the problem, Mr. Santori," she said, shooting to her feet. Hot, angry tears were building up in her eyes, and she would not allow herself to ugly cry in front of him. "This place is more than 'just business' to me. Owning my own coffee and bake shop is my *dream*, Mr. Santori. And I've worked my ass off for it. *You gave me your word*!"

"I ... I'm sorry, Sam. It's ... it's *business*."

"I'm sorry, too, Mr. Santori." Before she could say anything else she might regret, she grabbed her purse from behind the counter and went outside to wait for Steve.

~ *Anthony* ~

Anthony didn't turn around. He was dressed as a businessman today, using the reflection in his laptop screen to watch the scene unfold behind him.

Samantha was angry—and with good reason. The old man had swindled her!

Anthony remembered what this place had been like before Samantha came along. It had shit coffee and poor service. She'd worked hard to make it nice and welcoming again, and people around here loved her.

He loved her. Had from the very first moment she smiled at him. She was one of the few who had been kind to him. Who had looked beyond the surface and seen the real him.

Samantha got up and walked out. It was hard not to follow, but it wasn't time to reveal himself, not yet. And thanks to the selfish, scamming old lush, Anthony now had yet another chance to prove his love.

He knew what it was like to have a dream, then have it cruelly ripped away from you.

He had made the ones who had stolen his dreams pay. Now, he would make the old man pay for stealing hers.

CHAPTER SEVEN

~ Smoke ~

Smoke spotted Sam well before she saw him. Pacing up and down the sidewalk half a block away from the café, she didn't even seem to realize it had started to rain. Her delicate features were set in a glower, her lips moving faintly, as if she was talking to herself. Even pissed as she obviously was, the sight of her lifted his spirits. It was kind of hot actually, seeing her so worked up, though he would keep that opinion to himself.

"Sorry I'm late," he greeted her as he drew closer.

She stopped and lifted her head. It was then that he saw not only anger, but hurt, too. Unshed tears shimmered in her pretty eyes, making him want to fold her into his arms, and then kill whatever had put that look there. He didn't. Instead, he opened his umbrella and held it over her head.

"You okay?"

"Yes. *No*. Maybe."

"Did something else happen?"

"Yes," she said on an exhale. "But not what

you're thinking. It's … complicated."

"I'm a smart guy. Try me."

She thought about that for a moment, then nodded. "Okay, but on one condition."

"What's that?" he asked carefully.

"Not here. We talk over burgers and beer. My treat."

"Yes to the burgers and beer. Hell no on you treating. I pay, or I don't go."

One side of her mouth curled upward. "You're kind of a caveman, you know that?"

No argument from him there. "A fundamental element of Steve 101," he agreed.

"All right, but if I agree to that, then you have to let me take you to the store, so you can get a few essentials for your place. Like a coffeemaker." She smiled. "And garbage bags."

He hesitated. Not because he didn't need those things, but because her suggestion set warning bells tolling in his head. Shopping for housewares together seemed like such a domestic, coupley thing to do, and he wasn't mentally prepared for that. Granted, she had spent the night at his place, but under extenuating circumstances.

"Maybe."

"Fair enough."

Smoke pulled his hoodie up to cover his head as the rain went from a light drizzle to a steady fall. However, Sam scooted in closer, so they were both under the umbrella. He caught their reflection in a display window as they walked past and couldn't help noticing how right it felt. Maybe too right.

Again, he felt the ping of his internal trip wire, warning him that he might be unintentionally wading into unfamiliar and potentially dangerous territory. Wanting to help her out, being neighborly, and having lusty thoughts that he kept to himself— he was comfortable with those things. But *more* than that?

To further confuse things, his conscience reminded him that she was in a vulnerable place and he had to step carefully. She might misconstrue his desire to help as something more. Those waters were murky at best.

He liked her, sure. She was down-to-earth, nice to talk to, and appreciative of his efforts to help. Would he enjoy getting hot and sweaty between the sheets with her? Absolutely. But could he walk away in a couple of months with no hard feelings? Doubtful. She didn't seem like the type of woman to engage in a casual, no-strings kind of relationship, and he already felt more invested than he should at this stage.

What he did know was, he didn't want to hurt her. Until he figured out exactly what he was capable of and willing to give, he would proceed with extreme caution—for both their sakes.

Less than an hour later, they were in his Jeep, and Sam was directing him to a sketchy-looking place in the next town over.

When he parked and turned to her with a raised eyebrow, she simply said, "I know it doesn't look like much, but trust me, okay?"

The place—he didn't know the name of it because there was no sign—was small, dark, and packed. The interior was nicer than the exterior, but not by much. High-backed booths afforded privacy, and the low lighting lent the place a cozy feel.

Sam grabbed his hand and led him to a booth in the back. As his trained eyes scanned and analyzed their surroundings and the occupants, he tried not to think about how easily she had reached for him, nor how good her hand felt in his.

Sam slid in, and he took the seat across from her. He hoped the food was better than the decor. The ratty tablecloths and tacky plastic flowers didn't impress him, nor did the gruff server with half of her head shaved and tatted inspire confidence. But Sam had asked him to trust her, so he kept his thoughts to himself.

When he took a bite of his half-pound Angus burger and sampled the thick, hand-cut, seasoned fries fifteen minutes later, he admitted they were some of the best he'd ever had.

"I know you said you didn't like fast food, but I don't think this counts," she said, struggling to get her mouth around her own massive burger. "Andy's uses only meats from the local butcher shop, and the buns are baked fresh every day. Even the potatoes come from local farms."

"It's delicious," he agreed. "How did you find out about this place?"

"My grandparents owned a bakery. They provided the buns and breads for some local businesses, including this one. I used to deliver them every day before school."

"That explains your exemplary muffin-making skills."

She grinned, her face relaxed and pleasantly flushed. "I practically grew up in the bakery. After my mom's …" She cleared her throat and took a drink of her beer before continuing. "My mom had some issues, so my grandparents took me in and raised me. They were going to retire and let me take over after I got my degree."

He waited, sensing there was more to the story. He didn't have to wait long.

"But life has a way of messing with plans like that. They passed unexpectedly while I was still in college."

"I'm sorry. And taking over the business?"

"Wasn't going to happen," she finished. "The inheritance was only enough to keep a roof over my head and pay for college until I got my degree. I never gave up on my dream of having my own place though."

The server came by, and they ordered another round of the house draft, which, like the meals, was surprisingly good. Sam then told him about Santori, about the deal they had made, and what had happened earlier that day. It certainly explained why she had been so upset. Hell, it bothered *him*, and he wasn't directly affected by any of it.

"So," she said finally, pushing her half-empty plate away, "enough about me. You have more than enough material to ace Sam 101. What about you?"

Smoke was certain there was a lot more to Sam than what she had revealed, but she was clearly ready to change the subject. She looked at him expectantly with those big, pretty eyes, and once again, he felt their power deep in his chest.

He wasn't the sharing type, but there he was, telling her things he hadn't even told his brothers. Like how he had always wanted to be a SEAL, like his dad, who had died in action overseas when Smoke was a kid. He glossed over most of his military career for security reasons, which she seemed to understand, though he did talk about some of the places he had seen when they had some downtime.

An hour later, he was still talking, though he had directed the conversation away from him and to Church's vision.

"I remember the resort," she told him. "We used to supply their baked goods. It was a swanky place, really beautiful, and the owners were nice people. What happened there was such a tragedy."

"I don't know much about it," Smoke said honestly, "other than there was a fire."

"Oh, it was awful. The place was closed to the

public at the time, but nearly the whole family died that night. There was a son who survived. He was away at basic training or something."

Or BUD/S, Smoke thought.

"An arson investigator was brought in, but nothing ever came of it. At least, not as far as I know. Anyway, you guys are doing a wonderful thing. I'd love to help. I bet a lot of people in town would."

Sam meant well, and it was a nice idea, but whether to get the community involved in these early stages would be Church's call. As private as Smoke was, Church was even more so, and this project was extremely personal.

Eventually, the restaurant cleared out, and the server informed them they were closing. He paid the bill, gave the waitress a substantial tip—which earned him an actual smile and a thank-you—and then took Sam home.

She hesitated at her door. He knew she was still anxious about spending the night alone. After assuring him it would be the last time—they would see about that—she gratefully accepted his offer to crash at his place again.

"I'm sorry we didn't get to go shopping," she said, trying to suppress a yawn.

"I'm not," he replied honestly.

The hours they had spent together were pleasant, informative, and relaxed. His theory about Church's ties to the resort had been confirmed, and while he wouldn't have gone digging for the info, it wasn't exactly a national secret, not to the locals. Another plus: he had avoided the implied domesticity of picking out housewares together, which fell into line with his plan of proceeding with caution.

"You're such a guy," she murmured with a tired smile.

Within minutes, she was curled up on his recliner, breathing the deep, even breaths of slumber.

This time, despite the inner warnings and good intentions, he couldn't keep himself from pressing his lips to her forehead before he reluctantly turned in himself.

~ *Sam* ~

Sam woke up with a slight headache, most likely due to having that second beer. She wasn't used to drinking, and even two was enough to spawn a mild background throb and cottony morning mouth. It also explained last night's acute case of running mouth disease. That was the only thing that would have made her drone on about her personal life.

She *never* talked about her mother and rarely about her grandparents. Her mother because she didn't want anyone's pity. Her grandparents because, even years later, she still harbored some guilt about not being there when they'd needed her most. If life had followed her plan, she would have been living her dream, and her grandparents would have been enjoying their golden years down in Florida somewhere.

Poor Steve. He was a heck of a nice guy, and though he must have been bored to tears to hear her run on like that, he had been too kind to say so. But him, he'd had the most wonderful stories to tell. Tales of places and people she had only dreamed about. And listening to that deep baritone voice of his? She could have done that all night. He could have been reading an auto manual, and it would have sounded good to her.

She didn't have any illusions though. Denial wasn't really her thing. While his voice might soothe her ragged soul and his hard body might be spawning some steamy dreams, he clearly wasn't interested in anything beyond friendship. The moment of panic she had seen in his eyes when she casually mentioned picking up a few things for his apartment told her everything she needed to know.

That was fine with her. Mostly. When it came to her neighbor, her feelings were … complicated.

Steve was already awake, looking sexy and sleep-tousled. Sam decided this whole *friend zone* thing would be a lot easier if her heart didn't speed up and the area between her legs didn't throb at the mere sight of him, but what could she do?

Controlling what she said and did was one thing, but regulating her heartbeat and turning off the needy ache at will were beyond her abilities. She hadn't been able to shut down those warm tingles when she impulsively grabbed his hand at Andy's either.

She had to be careful. If he showed any kind of beyond-neighborly interest, she would be hard-pressed to refuse. Beneath the independent, capable front she tried to maintain, she was a closet romantic, and he was the closest thing to a modern-day knight in shining armor she'd ever encountered. No man had roused in her the same kind of undeniable attraction and interest that Steve had.

If the situation were different, she could easily see herself surrendering her body to him. Or worse, her heart.

"Good morning. Sleep well?"

His sexy, deep voice did nothing to alleviate the ache, she thought irritably. Weren't men the ones who were supposed to wake up aroused?

She avoided dropping her gaze to check that theory, opting to check her phone instead.

"Crap, I'm running late. I guess a night of bingeing will do that to you."

He laughed, the quiet rumble ratcheting up the ache in her core. "Two beers over the course of an entire evening? You call that bingeing?"

"It is for me," she told him. She focused on folding up the blanket she had used, placing it on the chair when it was a neat rectangle.

He followed her over to her place without asking, then checked the apartment while she brewed them each a cup of coffee. It occurred to her again how much she was coming to depend on him and how that might not be such a good thing. Especially when her feelings seemed hell-bent on rapidly progressing to *more than neighborly* despite her own internal warnings. She had to apply the brakes before she wrecked and dented them both.

"It's all good," he said a few minutes later, accepting the mug she handed to him.

"Thank you. Oh, and I forgot to mention … the locksmith is coming later today, so you can have your recliner back."

"I thought you said changing the locks wouldn't help. You're not still thinking of going to a motel, are you?"

"No, I can't afford that, especially not after what happened yesterday. If I can't change Mr. Santori's mind, I can't continue to work there. Money is going to be tight until I can find another job. I'll just have to pull up my big-girl pants and deal with it. I've imposed on you enough."

His eyes narrowed. "You're not imposing."

She continued as if he hadn't spoken. "You've gone above and beyond the good-neighbor code, and I just want you to know I appreciate it."

"What are you saying, Sam? That my services are no longer needed?" His voice was teasing, but his eyes were serious.

"What I'm saying, Steve, is that I hit a rough patch, you helped me through it, and I'm grateful. But this is my problem, and I have to deal with it."

When his eyes narrowed further, she felt the urge to squirm under his intense scrutiny but forced a sunny *I have this all under control now* smile until she thought her cheeks would crack.

"Go ahead and finish getting ready. I'll be back in fifteen to walk you to work."

His expression and tone dared her to challenge him, but she didn't. She'd said what she wanted to say, wanting him to know that she respected the boundaries of their friend zone and wasn't going to take advantage of his good nature or angle for something he wasn't ready or willing to give.

Since she would be providing him and his friends with coffee and muffins, she could rationalize him walking her to work as a *killing two birds with one stone* kind of convenient payback.

"Okay. Thanks."

With a final concerned glance over his shoulder, Steve left.

Sam looked out the window to check the weather. If it was still raining, she was going to carry her own umbrella today. Being that close to Steve and inhaling whatever spicy, clean scent clung to him would play havoc with her intention to keep things platonic.

The lingering cloud cover made it appear even

darker than usual, matching her mood. Unsurprisingly, she wasn't looking forward to going into the café. Yesterday, it had felt as if she were working toward something important. Today, it just felt like a job—and a thankless one at that.

Disappointed or not, she had a responsibility, and people were expecting her to be there. Until she figured out what she was going to do, there was no sense in burning bridges. If she quietly put the word out, maybe someone would have good leads on other places, other opportunities. Besides, the coffee shop hadn't officially been put up for sale yet. She still had a chance to change Mr. Santori's mind and convince him to do the right thing.

Sirens blared in the background as she took a quick shower and got dressed. She didn't think much of them since the firehouse was in the next block. It wasn't unusual to hear them going by at all hours of the day and night.

When she and Steve got closer to the café thirty minutes later, however, she realized where the engines had been going.

She watched in growing horror as the firefighters battled the flames licking skyward, smoke billowing from the broken windows of Santori's coffee shop.

They managed to contain the blaze before too long, but it was difficult to tell how much damage had been done.

The fire chief spotted her and came over to talk

to her.

"Chief Petraski, what happened?"

"That's what we're going to find out," the man said carefully. "Anything you can tell me, Sam?"

"No. I was just on my way in. Everything was fine when I left yesterday."

"You sure about that? I heard you and Mr. Santori had a disagreement."

Something in the chief's tone set her teeth on edge.

"You're not suggesting Sam had anything to do with this, are you, Chief?" Steve's voice was controlled, but Sam felt the tension rolling off him in waves.

"And you are?" the chief asked.

"Steve Tannen, the man who's been with Samantha since she left the bakery yesterday."

Chief Petraski's eyes turned back to her, assessing and questioning. "That right, Sam?"

It didn't take a psychic to know the thoughts going through the chief's mind, and she didn't particularly care for them.

"Yes," she said through gritted teeth. "Since my apartment was broken into two nights ago, Steve has been walking me to and from work and letting me crash on his recliner until I can get my locks changed."

The chief narrowed his eyes. "Break-in? Did you file a report?"

"Yes, of course I did."

"Hmpf," he muttered. No doubt he would be checking into that. "Want to tell me what you and the old man were arguing about before you left yesterday?"

"What does that have to do with anything?" Steve interjected.

"I don't like your tone, Mr. Tannen. Asking questions is part of conducting an investigation."

She felt Steve stiffen beside her. While she appreciated Steve's defense on her behalf, it wasn't helping the situation.

"Maybe you should just go, Steve," she said quietly. "The guys are expecting you."

"No, I think I'll stay right here," he said without taking his eyes off the chief. "This is more important."

She sighed. They would have to talk about personal boundaries later, but not in front of Chief Petraski.

She'd never been particularly fond of the chief, and she certainly didn't care much for his innuendos. Regardless, she'd done nothing wrong, and sooner or later, he would see that.

The rest of the morning passed by in a blur. True to his word, Steve remained by her side, a quiet, protective presence while she talked to the police, the fire chief, and curious customers, answering the same questions over and over.

Eventually, a patrolman brought Mr. Santori by in a police cruiser, but other than a few glances in her direction, the owner didn't acknowledge her. That hurt more than she wanted to admit. Mr. Santori couldn't possibly think she'd had anything to do with this morning's fire, could he?

"I don't like that fire chief," Steve said later. "Is he always an asshole, or does he have some personal beef with you?"

She almost smiled at his words. She wasn't used to someone rallying on her behalf. With Steve though, it seemed to come with the territory.

"You can't help it, can you?"

They sat in the back of the bustling diner, ten miles outside of Sumneyville. Her club sandwich remained untouched, her appetite nonexistent. Steve's assurance that she had been with him all night and all morning, suggestive as it was, was probably the only reason she was sitting here with him now instead of calling a lawyer from an interrogation room at the police station.

"Can't help what?"

"Rescuing people."

He seemed amused by the thought. "Is that what you think I'm doing?"

She nodded. "You escort me to and from work, give me a place to stay, provide an alibi." She tilted her head and looked at him thoughtfully. "What I can't figure out is, why would you do all that for me?"

He snorted. "Why wouldn't I?"

"Most people wouldn't."

"I'm not most people."

"Kinda my point. You hardly know me."

He looked away, as if suddenly uncomfortable. "Look, I don't have to know everything about you to know you didn't have anything to do with that blaze, and if Frick and Frack would get their heads out of their asses, they'd see it, too."

Her lips quirked at Steve's nicknames for the police and fire chiefs, who just happened to be brothers-in-law.

His words touched her though. It was nice to have someone believe in her, especially when people in the town obviously had their doubts.

"Sumneyville is a small town. Nepotism and drama are part of the local flavor."

"Doesn't make it right. Are you going to finish that?" he asked, changing the subject. When she shook her head, he signaled for the server. "Can you get us a box, please?" he asked politely.

The server—an attractive twenty-something who had unbuttoned an additional button, if not two, on her shirt when she realized Steve was sitting in her section—brought the box and the check.

Steve was a good-looking man. It was only natural women were attracted to him. Sam had to tamp down her simmering irritation though when she saw that *Lynnette* had signed the check with a heart and added her phone number on the back.

"Would you be so certain if we hadn't been together last night?" she asked plainly, saying it loud enough for Lynnette to overhear.

His eyes twinkled as if he knew what she was doing. "Yes," he said on a laugh.

"How can you be so sure?" she asked. "I was upset with Mr. Santori. There were eyewitnesses who were only too glad to say so."

"Sweetheart, you've got the killer instincts of a six-week-old puppy. You just don't have it in you to be that mean."

Sam didn't know what struck her more—the fact that the endearment had rolled so easily off his tongue or that he had compared her to a puppy.

"Now, come on. Grab your box, and let's go. There's something I want to show you."

~ *Anthony* ~

Anthony sat in his room, watching the video of the blaze on the news. He stared at the flames, mesmerized by the way they danced. *He* had made them dance like that.

He had always been drawn to fire. Its magnificent beauty. Its terrible power.

The elegance of the flames entranced him.

The camera didn't do them justice.

How he wished he could have stayed and watched them in person. Seen their brilliance command the darkness, felt their heat warm his skin, listened to the symphony of whooshes and crackles while they sated their hunger.

Fire was the ultimate element. It had the power to destroy. The power to cleanse.

So few understood that. Not even his mother had understood.

She used to cry sometimes, asking him to stop playing with fire. She had said she couldn't afford to keep moving, finding other schools when he let the fire out to play. When she had gotten the job at the resort, she had made him promise.

He'd tried—he really had. They had a nice place there, and there was plenty of space for him to run around even if he wasn't supposed to bother the guests. He liked hanging out in the kitchen, too. They had gas stoves and real wood-fired brick ovens. He would often sneak in to watch the flames as they danced for him.

Then, that nosy girl found him playing one day and said she was going to tattle …

She never did though. The fire had protected him even if it did leave him with scars.

He didn't feel bad about the people who had died. It was the girl's fault, not his. She was the one who had ruined everything. She thought being the owner's daughter made her better than everyone else. Better than him.

It hadn't.

He had learned a lot since then. Now, he could

command the fire. He was its master, and the flames obeyed him.

The café was his gift to Samantha. If it couldn't be hers, it wouldn't be anyone's.

CHAPTER EIGHT

~ *Smoke* ~

Sam was quiet on the trip up the mountain road. Every time he glanced over, she was staring out the window, lost in her own thoughts. She answered him pleasantly enough when he said something; otherwise, she didn't seem interested in conversation.

He couldn't blame her. It was a hell of a thing to be suspected of doing something like that—and by the very townspeople she served every day! He had been outraged on her behalf. Even if she was upset with the old man—and rightfully so—that was a shitty thing he had done. She just didn't have it in her to torch the place. If those Podunk chiefs shared half a brain between them, they would see that.

That was why he was making an exception to his usual "rules of separation" and taking her with him up to the site. Generally, he preferred to keep the various segments of his life separate. His work with Church and his former teammates was one segment. His apartment and his relationship with her was another. His personal history yet another. Organizing his life that way kept things neat and tidy. It was when one segment spilled into another that lines got blurred and boundaries were crossed.

He was crossing some serious boundaries with Sam, and, God help him, he wanted to obliterate a few of them.

Bringing Sam here felt right though. After the day she'd had, she could use a distraction, and quite honestly, he wasn't willing to leave her behind. He had already told her about the place, and she'd seemed really into it, so showing her felt like the next logical step. He didn't have to understand it. He was a man who had learned to trust and live by his instincts, and he wanted to share this with her.

"We're here." He pulled up and parked in the circular drive behind Mad Dog's flatbed, then hopped out and opened the passenger door for her.

"Are you sure about this, Steve?"

"Yeah, of course," he lied, still not a hundred percent certain that bringing her here was a good idea. Not only was he revealing another part of himself to her, but he was also revealing her to *them*. "Why wouldn't I be?"

She shrugged, looking past him to the stunning, if somewhat wild, view beyond. "I'm not sure I should be here. I feel like an intruder."

Had she somehow picked up on his thoughts? She did seem to have an uncanny ability to read him.

"Don't be ridiculous. You offered to help, remember? You should at least have some idea what you're getting into before you commit."

The words came out more like a warning than the tease he had intended. They were still talking about the resort renovations, right?

Her eyes came back to his, searching. She stared at him for long moments before finally saying, "I wouldn't have offered if I didn't mean it."

"What if it turns out to be more than you bargained for?"

She spoke slowly, as if carefully choosing her words. "Despite the last few days, I'm not some fragile flower. I appreciate the concern, but it's not necessary."

"I know it's not necessary. But that's what neighbors do, right? They look out for each other."

The moment the words were out of his mouth, he knew he'd said the wrong thing.

Her eyes shuttered, and she looked away again, choosing to look at something off in the distance instead of him. Then, her lips curled into a slight, enigmatic smile. "Yes, that's what neighbors do. And, not that you need it, but for as long as you're around, know that I'll have your back, too. So, do I get a tour or what?"

He reached for her hand, wanting to touch her, but she tucked her hands into her pockets and turned toward the manor house, pretending she hadn't seen it.

"Hey, Smoke! It's about time you got your fucking lazy ass up here," Mad Dog called from the doorway. "Oh, apologies, ma'am. Didn't see you there."

She laughed. "No apology necessary. I'm Sam. Steve was telling me about what you guys are doing here, and I practically begged him to let me tag along. I hope you don't mind," she lied, covering for him.

"Sam? As in the Sam who's been providing us with that nectar of the gods every morning?" Heff suddenly appeared out of nowhere. The shirtless bastard had his long, dark hair tied back, the diamond stud in his ear almost as bright as his megawatt smile. He sauntered up to Sam and kissed her hand. "These guys call me Heff, but you can call me anything you want."

She blushed. She fucking *blushed*.

An irrational rage washed over Smoke. He stepped up, put his hand on Heff's shoulder, and gave him a shove. "Knock it off, Casanova."

"Sorry, beautiful lady," Heff said, affecting a half-bow. "Didn't know you were spoken for."

"I'm not," she said quickly without even looking his way. "Steve and I are just neighbors."

Heff's grin grew wider before he held out his arm. "In that case, allow me to introduce you to everyone and show you around."

"I was just about to do that," Smoke said, his

voice coming out in a growl.

~ *Sam* ~

Sam stared at the gorgeous raven-haired guy who'd kissed her hand. Golden-tanned skin stretched over lean, cut muscles, accentuated by intricate tattoos adorning his chest and shoulders. A thin trail of fine, dark hair arrowed down and disappeared beneath a pair of jeans that sat low on his hips. Dark green eyes sparkled with mischief. She immediately pegged him as a player.

Steve stepped up closer to her, his body tense. If Sam didn't know better, she would swear Steve was being territorial, maybe even jealous, but that was probably a combination of her imagination and a bit of wishful thinking. His message that they were no more than friendly neighbors had come across loud and clear.

"That's okay, Steve," Sam said evenly. "You've already done so much."

Steve made another growly sound, but before he could say anything else, a man emerged from the building and garnered her attention. Taller than both Heff and Steve, he carried himself with the authority of a natural born leader. Shaggy chestnut-colored hair formed a perfect frame for his angled, masculine face. He looked different than the last time she had seen him, but she would remember those soulful golden-brown eyes anywhere.

"*Matt*? Matt Winston?"

His face was wary until he got closer. "Have we met?"

A tiny part of her was disappointed he didn't recognize her, but she couldn't blame him. The last time she had seen him, he had been the most popular guy in the senior class, and her freshman body hadn't yet developed enough to ever appear on his radar.

"My grandparents had a bakery. We used to provide some of the breads and baked goods for the resort. Even made a lot of the cakes for special occasions."

His eyes widened in recognition. "Sammy Appelhoff? Little Sammy?"

When she nodded, he pulled her into a hug, surprising her.

She laughed. "Not so little anymore."

He let her down and held her back to look at her. "I'll say."

She laughed again. "Looks like you've done some growing of your own. When Steve told me about what you guys were doing, I had no idea he was talking about you. Someday, you'll have to explain to me how you got the nickname Church because from what *I* remember, you were no choir boy."

He laughed but didn't bother denying it. "So, you're Smoke's neighbor, huh? I had no idea you were still around. How are your grandparents? Do they still have that bakery on Second Street? You wanted to take over the business, yeah?"

"I can't believe you remember that," she said, surprised. "But no. They passed when I was still in college."

"Shit. I'm sorry, Sammy. They were good people."

She nodded. "Your family were good people, too, Matt. It was awful, what happened."

A shadow fell over his face. Aware of the others watching them with interest, she sensed that was not a conversation he wanted to continue, so she said, "So, you're rebuilding, huh? I think that's awesome."

He nodded. "Bring it in, guys," he called. "Come meet an old friend of mine."

The others moved closer. In addition to Steve and the Lothario called Heff, there was a blond guy with nice hazel eyes, another with naturally wavy auburn locks and vivid green eyes, and the large, hulking guy who had shouted obscenities at Steve when they first arrived.

"Old friend, huh?" Blondie said with an easy, teasing smile.

Sam liked him immediately.

"Sammy, this is Doc." He pointed at Blondie. "Cage." He nodded at the auburn cutie. "And Mad Dog." He looked to the one called Heff, who smiled.

"We've already met."

"Why am I not surprised?" Matt said under his breath. "Guys, this is Sammy. Or do you prefer Samantha now?"

"Sam works."

"Sam it is. Do you have time to hang around for a while, or do you have to get back right away?"

"I have some time," she said. Time was pretty much all she had right now. "I'd love to have a look around, if that's okay."

"Of course. Give me a minute to rinse off and I'll take you on the grand tour."

"I'd like that," she said before Steve had a chance to object. "It'll give us a chance to catch up."

"How come he gets to play tour guide?" she heard Heff grumble.

"Because he's the boss," Doc answered.

"I'll be up at the main house. Let me know when you're ready to leave." Steve turned and stalked away before she could respond. He seemed angry, but she couldn't imagine why.

She chatted with the others until Matt returned.

"I forgot how beautiful it is here," Sam said, sitting on what remained of the old dock and looking out at the lake.

They had walked a good part of the perimeter, Matt explaining what he had planned for each phase. He didn't talk about the past, and she didn't bring it up. Losing loved ones in a tragic fire was something they had in common—even if he didn't realize that.

"You're doing a good thing here, Matt."

Matt leaned his hip against a sturdy-looking dock post. "Hope so," he said simply. "So … you and Smoke, huh?"

"It's not like that," she told him. "He's just helping me out a little, is all."

"Hmm …" he hummed thoughtfully.

"What's that supposed to mean?"

He ignored her question and asked one of his own. "What kind of help, Sam? Are you in trouble?"

"Nothing I can't handle," she said evasively.

"I've known Smoke a long time, Sam. Never known him to act without cause."

"Well, there's a first time for everything," she countered.

"All right, Sam. Message received loud and clear. I'll butt out."

They walked backed toward the main house.

"I think plenty of townspeople would be willing to get behind this project, myself included."

"Thanks, Sam. I appreciate that, but we got it covered."

She knew a *thanks, but no, thanks* when she heard one. "Okay. If you change your mind, you know where to find me."

They got back to the top just as the guys were finishing up for the day.

"Hey, Sam, we're heading into town to grab some dinner. Want to join us?" Blondie—Doc—asked.

She cast a look at Steve, who was staring earnestly somewhere else.

After everything that had happened that day—the fire, the questioning, Steve's "friend" talk, Matt's polite decline, and Steve's sulky demeanor—all she wanted to do was go back to her place and soak in a hot bath with a cup of tea, then curl up with a good book in her own bed.

"I'll pass, but thanks for the offer."

She climbed into the Jeep with Steve.

They were a couple of miles down the road when he said, "So, you know Church, huh?"

"Yes."

"Were you close?" He asked the question casually, but the muscles in his neck were tense.

Was that what was bugging him?

"No, not really. I'm surprised he even remembers me."

The rest of the ride was quiet. She didn't offer any additional information, and he didn't ask.

When he pulled into the parking lot, he said, "Listen, Sam, you should come out with us tonight."

He had said exactly what she'd wanted to hear, but not convincingly. The fact that he was staring out the window instead of looking at her confirmed it. He was being nice, but he didn't really want her there.

They had been spending a lot of time together. Maybe they were both due for a break. She knew she was. Her thoughts were a maelstrom of mixed signals and hurt feelings.

"Nah. I'm good."

"I'll stop by later when I get back."

"Don't bother," she said, climbing out of the Jeep. "I'll be asleep well before then. I'm beat."

A V formed between his brows. "You sure? What about the locks?"

"I got a text from the building manager. He said the locksmith was here this afternoon. It's all good. Thanks again for everything, Steve."

She moved toward the building, feeling Steve's eyes boring into her back the whole way.

She stopped by the building manager's office and picked up the new keys, then went up to her apartment.

"Oh, for heaven's sake," she murmured as she checked the sliding glass door.

Steve was standing outside his Jeep in the parking lot below, looking up at her. She gave him the thumbs-up sign and waved, then walked away. When she looked out again ten minutes later, he and his vehicle were gone.

~ *Anthony* ~

Anthony counted to ten before pulling out of the lot, making sure he stayed far enough behind the Jeep so he wouldn't be spotted.

At first, he had been angry when he discovered that she had changed her locks. It meant he would have to play the role of maintenance man again, and that building manager was starting to get suspicious.

That wouldn't be a concern for much longer. Things were almost ready. He couldn't wait to surprise her!

Something would have to be done about G.I. Joe though. He had been spending far too much time with Samantha. Anthony knew it wasn't her fault; the guy was just too dense to take a hint.

Anthony was going to take care of that, too.

CHAPTER NINE

~ *Smoke* ~

What the hell just happened?

The words played on repeat as he pulled out of the parking lot and headed out to meet up with the guys. As far as he knew, nothing had been done or said that explained the subtle void in his chest.

Sam just blew you off.

Well, there was that.

Granted, her day had ranked fairly high on the *crappy day* meter, but his gut told him there was more to it. This last week, when something worrisome had happened, she had turned *to* him, not *away* from him.

Maybe it has something to do with the mixed signals you've been putting out there, genius.

Those signals might have been mixed, but they were an accurate reflection of what was going on inside his head.

Sam might think he was some kind of white knight, but any armor he wore was dented and tarnished. When he was taking care of her or working on the resort, he didn't have to deal with his own issues. His mind was quieter. The flashbacks, the brief but debilitating moments of panic, were practically nonexistent.

As if on cue, that familiar sensation of being trapped squeezed his chest. He put the windows down and inhaled deeply, forcing himself to remain calm. He was INCONUS—inside the continental US—not in some underground pit halfway across the world. The darkness around him came from the evening sky, not the heavy slabs of rocks that had kept him hidden from the ones looking for him. The air he drew into his lungs was scented with mountain pine, not his own filth.

Those thoughts helped to keep the worst of it at bay. What helped *more* was picturing Sam curled up on his recliner, a soft smile on her lips after whispering his name in her sleep. Remembering the gentle warmth of her petite hand in his. Seeing those pretty gray-green eyes looking at him as if he was something special. He wasn't, but it was nice that she thought he was.

By the time he reached Franco's, Smoke had himself under control again.

Doc waved his hand from the back corner, where they had pushed a couple of tables together. Unsurprisingly, Mad Dog was already working his way through an enormous plate of wings.

Smoke signaled the server as he sat down, receiving a nod and a friendly smile in return. Sandy was cool. Friendly, but not overly so, and she took good care of them.

"Where's Sam?" Heff asked, looking toward the door, as if expecting her to follow.

That annoyed him. Smoke didn't want Heff setting his sights on Sam.

"She's not coming."

"Why not? Didn't scare her off, did you?"

Maybe. "She had a rough day."

"We weren't that hard on her. Unless Church was." Heff grinned. "What kind of tour did you give her, Church? Did you show her how you got your nickname?"

Beneath the table, Smoke's fists clenched. Heff was just being Heff, trying to get a reaction.

Church had gotten his nickname one night when they were still wet behind the ears. They had gone out, overindulged, and Church ended up sleeping with a local preacher's daughter. Her cries to the Almighty had kept the rest of them up most of the night, and the nickname had stuck.

That memory usually came with a smile, but not this time.

Smoke shifted his gaze to Church, remembering the way he had hugged Sam. A sharp pain lanced through his belly, the same one he'd felt when he watched them disappear over the hill together.

Church met his gaze head-on, as if reading Smoke's dark thoughts. Amusement flickered there along with the assurance Smoke had been hoping to find. *Not like that, man*, it said. That was good enough for him.

"Earth to Smoke," Cage said, snapping his fingers. "This wouldn't have anything to do with what you asked me to look into, would it?"

He looked at Cage, at all the guys who were now giving him their full attention.

"Smoke," Church said, his amusement fading, "what's going on?"

Smoke thought briefly about offering a denial, but they wouldn't buy it. Church and Heff knew him too well, and the others were sharp enough to detect a lie.

Smoke wasn't one to go around sticking his nose in other people's business, and he didn't make a habit of asking Cage or anyone else for favors off the clock. Though they had hidden it well, he had sensed their shock when he showed up at the site with Sam. Maybe they could help. As SEALs, they had always worked better as a team than alone.

Their food arrived, and Sandy brought his beer along with refills for everyone else. Well, everyone, except Heff, who was deliberately avoiding her gaze, which meant things hadn't changed much. His teammate was still a manwhore.

As they ate, Smoke filled them in on Sam's situation. He told them about the weird gifts and the break-ins as well as the present he had found in his own bathroom. When he got to the fire, Church's face went blank.

"Jesus," Cage muttered. "It can't be a coincidence."

"What can't be a coincidence?"

"Did Sam tell you how her grandparents died?"

"No," he said. He had a feeling he wasn't going to like whatever Cage had to tell him.

"They lived in an apartment above their bakery. They died of smoke inhalation when a fire broke out in the kitchen below."

"Sam said she was at college when her grandparents passed."

"According to Sam's official statement, she was."

Something about the way Cage had said that made cold ice slither down the length of his spine. There was more Cage wasn't saying, and while Smoke might not want to hear it, he had to.

"But …" he prompted.

"But … Sam's roommate spent the night with her boyfriend and couldn't corroborate Sam's statement that she was there all night."

"So?" This was from Mad Dog, who had stopped eating and was now fully engrossed in the discussion.

"So, a neighbor swore she saw someone skulking around the bakery in the middle of the night."

"Again, I ask, so?"

"Sam's place wasn't that far away. It was close enough that she could help out at the bakery and commute to classes. Apparently, Sam had some kind of scarf she was particularly fond of—wore it all the time. The neighbor swears that whoever she saw that night was wearing that scarf. When questioned about it, Sam said that scarf was missing. Either she'd lost it or someone had snatched it."

"Convenient," Doc muttered.

Smoke shook his head. "It doesn't make sense. Sam's dream is to have a place of her own. She said her grandparents were going to retire and turn the place over to her once she got her degree. Why would she sabotage her own future?"

"Insurance," Cage answered. "The bake shop was old, in need of renovation. It would have taken a small fortune to modernize. The grandparents had a substantial policy on the place, more than enough to rebuild. Unfortunately, the cause of the fire was suspicious, and when the fire chief refused to rule out arson, the insurance company wouldn't pay out. As the sole beneficiary, Sam was left with only a meager nest egg—enough to finish school and live modestly, if she was careful."

"Sam, a firebug? No way." Smoke refused to believe Sam was capable of anything like that. However, it did explain why the fire and police chiefs had been so keen on questioning her.

"What do you think, Church? You knew her, didn't you?" This was from Doc.

"I knew her," Church said slowly, brows drawn

tight over his eyes, as if deep in thought. "But we weren't that close. She was nice, always friendly, on the quiet side."

"That doesn't make her an arsonist!" Smoke said vehemently.

"No, it doesn't," he agreed. He pinned Cage with a look. "In any of your research, did the name Anthony Cavatelli come up?"

"Doesn't ring a bell. Why?"

"His mother worked at the resort. They lived in one of the smaller cabins, the ones for staff who didn't want to live in town. They were there the night"—Church cleared his throat—"the night of the fire. His mother's body was found in the kitchen. Anthony was discovered unconscious just outside the door, with burns over half his body."

"You think they had something to do with it?" Mad Dog guessed.

"When he woke up, the kid said he'd snuck into the kitchens because he was hungry. He turned on a burner to make himself a grilled cheese or something, and the next thing he knew, he was waking up in the burn ward."

"But you don't think it was an accident, do you?" asked Mad Dog.

"No," Church said, his face grim. "My sister used to write to me every week after I enlisted. She talked about this weird kid who played with lighters all the time and gave her the creeps."

"Anthony Cavatelli," Doc murmured.

Church nodded. "She said he used to follow around pretty young girls who were staying there with their families. My parents received a few complaints and talked to the mother about it, who admitted the kid had some issues. She said he was harmless but that she'd keep closer tabs on him and make sure he took his meds."

"What became of him?"

"Don't know." Church frowned. "I got emergency leave to take care of things, but I couldn't stick around long afterward. Last I heard, they put him in a state facility for evaluation and were looking for relatives. I lost track after a while. But he was only about thirteen then, so I'm sure all those records are sealed."

"The fire was about ten years ago, so that would make him about twenty-three now, right?" Doc asked. "Which means he could have conceivably gotten out about five years ago. When did Sam's grandparents' place burn?"

"Five years ago," Cage replied.

"Fuck," grunted Mad Dog.

"I heard her say her grandparents used to provide baked goods to the resort," Heff said, speaking up for the first time. "What if she's one of those pretty girls Anthony followed around? She's nice to him, he's smitten, so he decides to look her up when he comes back to town."

Doc picked up the thread. "So, he goes to the grandparents', only to find out that Sam doesn't live there anymore. Maybe they don't give him her info, and he lashes out by torching the place. Then, he bides his time, becomes her secret admirer, sends her gifts, follows her around, just waiting for the right moment to reintroduce himself."

"Then, you show up." Cage pointed to Smoke. "He sees you as competition and steps up his game. Maybe even hears what Santori did and decides to avenge her or some shit like that."

Church looked at Cage. "Can you get into those sealed records and find out exactly what Cavatelli's issues were?"

"No, but I know someone who can," Cage said. "An old buddy of mine. He can hack into anything."

"Think he'll help?" Doc asked.

"Hell yes, especially if he finds out why we're asking. The guy's got a bigger soft spot for damsels in distress than our own Smoke here," he said with a grin. "Sealed juvie records will be a piece of cake for him. While he's working on that, I can run some searches on Anthony Cavatelli and see what hits we get. Maybe find a picture or something we can show to Sam, see if she recognizes him."

"I don't know," Heff mused. "It all seems kind of fucked up."

"Yeah, it's fucked up," Smoke agreed, "but it fits."

Which meant that Anthony, or whoever was stalking Sam, had been keeping close tabs on her and probably knew she was home alone at that very moment.

"I gotta go."

"You want us to come with?" Church asked.

"No, but hang tight. I'll call if I need you."

"You got it."

~ *Sam* ~

"Gah!" Sam lifted up her head and punched her pillow in an effort to make it more comfortable.

After two nights on Steve's recliner, she'd thought getting some sleep in her own bed would be a no-brainer, but no. Sleep continued to prove elusive. Physically, she was exhausted, but mentally, she was doing sprints.

An image of Steve's soulful, concerned eyes as she got out of his Jeep seemed to have been cut and pasted onto the backs of her eyelids. Each time she closed her eyes, all she could see was that look. She had no idea what it'd meant or what he had been thinking, but it made her soul ache.

What she did know was that she felt bad about putting that look in his eyes. She'd known him less than a week, yet he had been nicer to her than ninety-nine percent of the people she had known far longer.

How many others would have walked her to and from work every day? Let her crash on their recliner? Stuck by her side when the people of her own hometown suspected her of setting fire to Mr. Santori's coffee shop?

Granted, Steve didn't know what had happened to her grandparents' bakery; he hadn't been around long enough to hear the rumors still circulating, even now. He knew she was innocent in this case because she had been with him all night. But what if she hadn't? Would he still be championing her?

She gave up on her plan to make an early night of it and went to the kitchen. The calming herbal tea and hot bath hadn't worked, so perhaps it was time for a classic—warm milk with vanilla. Her grandmother used to make it for her when she had trouble sleeping as a child, and it had worked wonders then.

While the milk warmed on the stove, she wandered over to the window and looked down at the lot below. Was Steve back yet? Would he heed her directive to not stop by? She hadn't heard him come in, but he was pretty quiet. A brief scan showed that his Jeep wasn't there.

He and his friends were probably having a good time. They seemed to be a close bunch, almost like family. She supposed that happened when you lived and worked together as a team like they did, relying on each other and literally trusting one another with their lives. She envied them that.

Besides her mother, her grandparents had been the only family she had. However, while they had taken her in and given her everything she needed, they hadn't been overly affectionate.

They had come to America as immigrants, real-life examples of the American dream. Hard work was more important than hugs, and with owning a business, working sixteen-to-twenty-hour days left little time for fun.

Between school and helping out at the bakery, she didn't have many friends. She didn't have the time or the money for silly, frivolous things, like going to the movies or football games or proms, and that tended to put a damper on teenage social life.

She had learned a lot though. Her framed degree looked nice on the wall, but most of her business knowledge had come from real-life experience. Working those long hours had exposed her to every aspect of running a bake shop—from doing the books to handling customers and everything in between, including loading and driving the delivery truck. That was why she had done so well in turning around Mr. Santori's coffee shop. That was also how she *knew* she could be a success with her own place, *if* she ever got the chance.

Unfortunately, it didn't look like that was going to happen anytime soon. Tomorrow, she was going to have to start looking for another job. Maybe even in another town. She would be hard-pressed to find someone willing to hire her in Sumneyville after what had happened this morning. Small towns had long memories, and the truth wasn't as important as what people believed or what they *thought* they knew.

Sam turned off the kitchen light and moved over to the sofa with her warm milk, tucking her feet up beneath her.

Rather than lose herself in those depressing thoughts, she went back to thinking about Steve and reflecting on the more positive parts of the day. Like how he'd stood up for her in front of Fire Chief Petraski and Chief of Police Freed and held her hand in a show of support. And how he had taken her up to the site and introduced her to his friends rather than leave her to sulk alone in her apartment.

Maybe he didn't feel the same kinds of things for her that she had begun to feel for him, but his actions proved that he *did* care. Maybe, in time, the easy connection between them would become something more, or maybe it wouldn't. Either way, she would be a fool to throw away the chance.

Sam made up her mind then and there. No more worrying about what would and wouldn't happen. People were going to believe what they wanted to believe. The most she could do was hold her head high and trust that the evidence would tell the real story. As far as Steve was concerned, she would take each day as it came. If Steve just wanted to be friends, then she was going to be a damn good one.

Starting now.

She sprang up from the couch.

The coffee shop was closed indefinitely, but that didn't mean she couldn't still make treats for Steve and the guys. She started pulling out everything she needed—flour, sugar, cocoa, baking powder, eggs, oil. She was running low on vegetable oil. Should she make a quick trip to the store for more?

She checked the clock. It was almost ten. The grocery store was closed, but the twenty-four-hour mini-mart might have some. Sam threw on a pair of comfortable workout pants and a light jacket. Her hand was on the doorknob when she froze.

Was she really thinking about heading out alone at ten o'clock at night, knowing someone might be stalking her?

The mini-mart was only a few blocks away, and the area was generally well-lit, but maybe it wasn't the smartest idea, given the circumstances. Besides, with the way her luck had been running lately, something would catch on fire along the way, and she would be suspected of that, too.

Gah! She hated this! Hated having to worry about leaving her own apartment to do something as normal as running to the store for vegetable oil.

She dropped her purse and took off her jacket with a heavy sigh.

Things would get better. The authorities would find out who had really set that fire, and whoever was stalking her would be caught. She had to believe that. In the meantime, she would just have to stay smart and make the best of it.

"Applesauce instead of oil it is," she muttered to the empty space around her, then pulled out her stand mixer and got started.

~ *Anthony* ~

Anthony pulled on the lumpy body suit, followed promptly by some oversize stockings that gathered at the ankles and a dress he had picked up at the thrift store. The formless flower-print monstrosity was hideous and smelled like mothballs, which was precisely why he had chosen it. Glasses were next, as were a pair of gaudy, faux clip-on pearl earrings, followed by the bluish-gray wig of short curls to complete the ensemble.

He appraised himself in the mirror. The heavy pancake makeup did a good job of concealing his five o'clock shadow. In retrospect, he probably should have shaved, but disabling G.I. Joe's Jeep had taken longer than anticipated.

Oh well. It didn't matter now. The task was done. In a matter of hours, G.I. Joe would be out of the picture, and he and Sam would be beginning their new life together.

Anthony grinned, adjusted his denture overlay, and slipped the little bottle of chloroform into his handbag.

Showtime. It would be Mrs. Himmelwright's final performance.

CHAPTER TEN

~ *Smoke* ~

Smoke couldn't get out the door fast enough. He jumped into his Jeep and dialed Sam's number. She answered on the third ring.

"Sam? It's Steve. Is everything all right there?"

"Yes, Steve, everything is fine."

"Good. That's good." He closed his eyes in relief.

"Are *you* okay?" she asked. "Did you meet up with the guys?"

"Yeah, I'm fine. And, yes, I did. I'm just leaving."

"Are you okay to drive?"

He smiled at the concern in her voice. When was the last time someone other than his teammates had given a shit? "Yeah, I'm good. Listen, I know it's kind of late, but I'd like to stop by when I get back, if that's okay. There's something I want to talk to you about."

She didn't hesitate. "Okay."

"You sure you don't mind?"

"I'm sure. I'm making muffins."

His grin grew. He could just picture Sam in the kitchen, smudges of flour on her nose and fingers. He pushed those thoughts away when he started getting hard.

"Then, I'll definitely be there. See you in about twenty?"

"Okay."

He disconnected the call and started up the Jeep. Hearing Sam's voice eased some of his worries, but that sense that something was wrong was still there, tugging persistently.

Ten minutes later, it had become so bad that his heart was pounding and his knuckles glared white against the black steering wheel.

Some of the symptoms were similar, but this wasn't one of his flashbacks. Rather than debilitating him, they were urging him to action.

He pressed the Bluetooth button on the console and spoke the verbal command to dial Sam's number. After a moment, the ring could be heard over the vehicle's speakers.

It rang once, then twice.

"Come on," he muttered. "Pick up."

Three rings, then four before a digital female voice said, "Please leave a message," followed by a beep.

"Sam, it's Steve again. I'm on my way. Don't open the door for anyone but me, okay? And call me back as soon as you get this."

He disconnected and applied pressure to the

accelerator, no longer simply surpassing the posted speed limit, but shattering it.

Flashing blue lights appeared in his rearview mirror, eliciting a string of muttered profanities.

Stopping now wasn't an option. The sense of impending danger was nearly overwhelming. He was only five minutes out from the apartments, less if he kept up this pace.

He downshifted and stepped on the brakes to make the turn. Less than a second later, the resistance beneath his foot disappeared entirely, and the pedal slammed down to the floorboard.

"Fuck!" What the hell had happened to his brakes?

Smoke was an accomplished driver, but at the speed he was going, no amount of skill was going to get his Jeep around the turn without rolling it.

He shot past the turnoff, his years of training taking over. He calmed his mind and concentrated on staying on the road and avoiding other cars while considering his options.

The answer came in the form of a dairy farm half a mile later. With the cops still on his tail, Smoke downshifted again, then yanked the wheel, veering the Jeep off the road.

With the gears grinding in protest, the big tires hit the soft soil and lurched to the side, causing Smoke to bang his head … hard. That slowed his forward momentum, but it didn't stop it entirely.

Blood poured into his left eye. He blinked it

away and focused on the moonlit landscape, looking for something to slow his roll with minimal risk of injury.

A big red barn loomed ahead and was getting bigger by the second. Jerking sharply to the left, he maneuvered the bouncing vehicle away from the barn, realizing his mistake too late when he saw what appeared in his headlights.

Smoke pulled hard on the emergency brake and braced for impact.

~ *Sam* ~

Sam pulled up the classic rock station on her music streaming app and turned up the volume, moving her hips to the beat. Measure, mix, measure, crack, mix. The motions were familiar, comforting.

A flutter seemed to have taken up residence beneath her rib cage. She couldn't help it; she was looking forward to seeing Steve. Now that she had accepted the fact that she felt more than friendship for him as well as the knowledge that they would keep things in the friend zone for the foreseeable future, some of the weight had lifted off her shoulders.

Self-denial and worrying about what someone else did or didn't feel was exhausting. The heart wanted what it wanted, and she could no sooner change what she felt than he could. What she *could* do was just be herself, make the most of each moment, and see where things went. Whatever happened, happened.

A knock at the door got her attention. *He's here!*

"Just a minute," she called out. She put the spooned batter into the last cup and slid the tin into the preheated oven.

She was just setting the timer when the knock was repeated, louder and more insistent.

"I'm coming!" she called out again, a smile curving her lips.

What was it about men and baked goods? Maybe that old saying really was right—the way to a man's heart was through his stomach. If that was the case, she thought with a chuckle, she might actually have a chance with the sexy, chivalrous SEAL.

Sam opened the door, surprised to find not Steve, but her neighbor, Mrs. Himmelwright.

"I'm sorry, dear," Mrs. Himmelwright said in her croaky voice, wringing her hands as the scents of mothballs and arthritis cream hit Sam head-on. "I seem to have locked myself out of my apartment again, and I heard your music. Do you mind if I borrow your phone to call the building manager? He's not in his office."

Sam held the door, her neck prickling with unease. *Jeez!* How paranoid was she if the sight of her elderly neighbor had her guard up?

"Uh, sure, of course. Let me grab it for you. I have it right over here on the counter."

"Ooh … something smells wonderful," her neighbor said, stepping inside the apartment and looking around in interest. "Are you baking?"

"Yes. It helps me unwind." Sam's unease intensified. She hadn't invited Mrs. Himmelwright in and was annoyed the elderly woman had entered anyway. Maybe it was rude, but Sam didn't like people in her living space. Well, except for Steve. She didn't mind when he was here.

She reached for her phone, anxious to call the building manager and send Mrs. Himmelwright on her way. With any luck, he would be quick to respond, and Mrs. Himmelwright would be back in her own place before Steve arrived.

Sam no sooner had the phone in her hand than a cloth was pressed over her nose and mouth. She tried to scream and twist away, but the arm wrapped around her waist was surprisingly strong.

A sickeningly sweet scent filled her mouth, and her vision grew cloudy.

"Don't fight it, Samantha," a decidedly masculine voice said. "Everything is going to be all right now."

CHAPTER ELEVEN

~ *Smoke* ~

There's nothing like a stack of wrapped hay bales to stop a runaway vehicle, Smoke thought wryly. His head hurt like a bitch, but he boxed up the pain and shoved it into the back of his mind. He had survived far worse.

Luckily, he had managed to angle the vehicle so he hadn't hit head-on.

A few good shoves of his shoulder, and he was able to get the door open enough to stumble out. Tiny stars danced across his vision while he regained his sense of balance.

No, not tiny stars. Flashlights.

The cops who had been trying to pull him over were now making their way across the field, and if their angry shouts were any indication, they weren't happy with the car chase.

"Knees on the ground! Hands where we can see them!"

It was impossible to see beyond the blinding beams, but he bet at least one of those yahoos had his firearm out and pointed in his direction.

Smoke went down on his knees and put his arms up. "Can you shine that somewhere else, please?"

"You drunk, boy?"

Smoke recognized the voice as one of the cops who had come out to Sam's the night of the break-in. Typical small-town police officer—older, paunchy, with an inflated sense of self-importance.

"No. The brakes went out on my Jeep."

The cop chuckled, more in disbelief than humor. "That so?"

"You think I like driving across cornfields and crashing into things?"

"Well, now, maybe our little town isn't exciting enough for you."

"He's got blood all over his face, Joe. Maybe we should take him to the hospital or something." That was from the younger guy, the one who looked fresh out of the academy and was at least trying not to come across as a total douche.

"Nah. He doesn't need a hospital. He's a tough guy, aren't you, Tannen?"

Smoke ground his teeth together. He didn't know what kind of grudge they had against him, but he didn't have time for this shit. He needed to get to Sam.

"I don't need a hospital. I need to get back to my apartment building. Sam might be in danger."

"Sam? You mean, the girl who called us because someone sent her flowers?" This time, they both laughed. "What's wrong? Did a fruit basket show up on her doorstep today?"

Smoke tried to hold his temper in check, but it wasn't easy. It would take less than two seconds to disable both of these men, secure them with their own handcuffs, and leave them in the trees for someone else to find. As satisfying as that would be, he would only do that as a last resort.

"Can I put my hands down now?"

"Yeah, but put them behind your back, so Lenny here can cuff you. Keep you from getting any funny ideas."

Trying to reason with them was like talking to two of The Three Stooges.

"Are you going to take me to check on Sam and make sure she's safe?"

"The only place you're going, pal, is down to the station to sleep it off."

They had officially reached the last resort.

Smoke leaned to the side, sweeping out his leg in an arc and catching both men off guard. Seconds later, he had disarmed them both and left them cuffed to each other, back to back, with a fence post between them.

"Sorry about this, guys," he said as he took the clips out of their guns and tossed them out of reach. "I did try to be reasonable, but I don't have time to play games. My woman's life might be in danger."

My woman.

The words made him pause, but there was no

denying the truth of them. From the moment he'd met Sam, he'd felt compelled to look out for her, his gut recognizing what his mind wasn't ready to accept—Sam *was* his, had been since the first time she flashed those pretty eyes his way. Those same instincts were now urging him to get his ass moving with all the subtlety of an air raid siren.

Neither officer responded. When they woke up, they were going to be pissed. Plus, he would have a double shot of assaulting a police officer added on to whatever list of trumped-up charges they could come up with between them. He would deal with that later. Getting to Sam and ensuring she was safe was his priority.

Smoke grabbed his phone from the front seat of his Jeep and called Sam. Once again, the call went to voice mail. He tried Church next, giving him a quick rundown of the situation. Church agreed to meet him at his place.

The police cruiser had been left running— something he knew officers did to keep the in-vehicle computers online. He slipped behind the wheel, turned off the lights, and made his way back to the road.

The next call that came over the police scanner nearly stopped his heart.

"All units in the vicinity. Smoke reported at Sumneyville Apartment complex, 2173 Spruce Street. Engine and ambulance en route."

Smoke pressed down on the accelerator,

offering up prayers and barters that he wouldn't be too late. By the time he got there, volunteer fire and police already had the road blocked off.

Smoke pulled off to the side and jumped out a block away. Flashing lights lit up the area in splashes of red and blue. The fire engine was in front of his building, the local ambulance parked not far away. Curious onlookers gathered along with evacuated tenants, chattering nervously as they watched from across the street.

Smoke rushed around to the parking lot side and looked up, his heart falling further when he saw smoke coming out of an apartment on the seventh floor. Sam's apartment.

He ignored the stares at his bloodstained face and shirt as he searched for Sam among the crowd. There was only one face he wanted to see, and it wasn't there.

"Smoke." Church's voice cut through the din.

Smoke looked around to find Church, Heff, and Doc appearing suddenly, as if out of nowhere.

Doc's eyes immediately went to the gash on his head. "You okay there, Smoke?"

"Yeah, looks worse than it is."

Doc narrowed his eyes but thankfully accepted his self-assessment. Or more likely, he realized there were more important concerns at that moment.

"You find Sam yet?"

"No, and her car's still in the lot. I need to get inside." Smoke turned his gaze upward. "The smoke's coming out of her place."

Church nodded. "Doc, go with him. Heff and I will take another look around down here."

The volunteer fireman positioned at the back entrance was just a kid. He gave a half-hearted protest when the two men informed him they would be going upstairs, then stood down when he saw they weren't going to quietly walk away.

"Looking pretty fierce there with that blood all over your face," Doc commented as they double-timed it up the stairs. "You might want to wipe some of that off before Sam sees you."

"That bad?" Smoke asked when they reached the seventh floor.

"Not if you're auditioning for the prom scene in *Carrie*."

"Shit." Smoke took the bandana Doc held out to him and did a quick swipe. "Better?"

"It'll do. You're going to need stitches."

"Later."

Firemen dressed in gear were coming out of Sam's apartment. One guy took one look at the two of them and held up his hand. "You shouldn't be here."

"It's all right," said a deeper voice behind him. "It's all clear. *You*," the fire chief said, his eyes narrowing when he saw who it was, "is this your apartment?"

"No," Smoke said carefully. Apparently, the fire chief didn't realize the place belonged to Sam.

It also meant that Sam wasn't there. "I live in the one next to it."

"Well, it's your lucky day, Mr. Tannen. We were able to contain the blaze before it spread, so you still have a place to sleep tonight."

"Do you know what caused the blaze?"

Chief Petraski's eyes narrowed. "Muffins, left in the oven. Who lives in this apartment?"

"How should I know? I just moved in last week. Haven't had the welcome mixer yet."

"I'd watch myself if I were you, Mr. Tannen."

"Noted. Can I get into my place now? It's been a rough night."

The chief looked like he wanted to say more, but didn't.

Smoke felt his eyes on his back as he opened the door. After Doc followed him in, he shut the door behind him and waited.

"Looks like you make friends wherever you go, Smoke."

"That's one of the douchebags who was giving Sam a hard time," Smoke told him.

"Yeah, I figured as much. Why don't you go change and clean yourself up while we wait for them to leave? Can't do much with them here."

Smoke would much rather be in Sam's apartment, looking for something that would tell him what had happened and where she had gone. There was no way Sam would have just upped and left in the middle of baking like that without a damn good reason, not when she knew he was on his way.

If he thought for one moment that Chief Petraski would actually listen, he would bring him up to speed, but the chief had already proven incapable of being objective when it came to Sam. Besides, while the Anthony Cavatelli theory made perfect sense, they had absolutely nothing in the way of supporting evidence. No, they were going to have to handle this themselves until they had viable proof.

By the time he took a quick shower, changed, and slapped some butterfly tape on his head wound, the last of the firemen were leaving. He and Doc waited until the hallway was quiet, then went next door. Ignoring the yellow tape across the door and the *By Order of the Fire Marshal* post affixed to the door, they picked the lock and were inside in less than a minute.

Smoke looked around, his chest tight. The acrid stench of smoke filled the space along with the chemical scent of whatever extinguisher they had employed. The door to the oven hung open, the twisted metal pan holding the charred, blackened remains of the muffins. Canisters of flour and sugar sat open on the counter along with a jar of applesauce and a half-full carton of eggs.

He knew Sam wasn't there, but he looked around anyway, searching for some clue of what might have happened.

Sam's lightweight jacket still hung on a hook

by the door, her purse beneath it. A quick check showed her wallet was still there, as were her keys.

"Hey, Smoke, over here." Doc was crouched down, reaching under the small breakfast bar that doubled as a table. "Recognize this?"

It was Sam's phone. Smoke took it from Doc and saw his two missed calls. A few swipes showed no texts or calls between the time she had talked to him and then.

"Where the hell are you, Sam?"

CHAPTER TWELVE

~ *Smoke* ~

Smoke's phone signaled an incoming call. He reached for it, hoping to hear Sam's voice but heard Church's instead.

"Heads-up, Smoke. The police chief is headed your way, and he doesn't look happy. Take the back way. We'll meet up on the north side of the park in five. Cage called. You're going to want to hear what he has to say."

When Smoke and Doc jogged up less than five minutes later, Cage and Mad Dog were already there, their expressions serious.

"Tell him," Church commanded.

Cage's face was grim. "A couple of months after his release from the psychiatric facility, Cavatelli popped up in Brenner's Gap, a town about twenty miles from here. He got a job in the local community theater there. The place closed up shortly afterward."

"Let me guess," Smoke said. "A fire?"

"Ding, ding, ding! Give the man a cookie. The theater went up in flames after a performance.

Luckily, no one was around."

"So, what happened to Cavatelli?"

"No one knows. He just vanished." Cage shrugged. "I'll put another call in to my friend, tell him to put a rush on those juvie records. Maybe he'll be able to find something I missed."

"Shit. Don't you have any good news?"

"Well, I did manage to get a hit on that partial plate, but I'm not sure if you'll consider it good news or not. The only vehicle with those numbers matching the make and model you saw is registered to an eighty-two-year-old woman named Constance Himmelwright, who just happens to live on the same floor as you and Sam."

Smoke frowned. He knew Mrs. Himmelwright. She scowled at him every time he saw her in the hallway. "That definitely wasn't an eighty-two-year-old woman I saw pointing a cell phone my way."

"You're right about that," Cage agreed, tapping a few buttons on his laptop. "And the security camera covering that section of the lot agrees with you." He turned the laptop so the screen was facing them. "Male, Caucasian, looks about the right age to be our guy. The image isn't crystal clear, but it should be enough to feed into a good facial recognition program and compare it with any photos we can dig up."

"Will that work?"

"People age, but their bone structure doesn't

change. I've got some kick-ass software. If we can dig up a photo of Cavatelli, even an old one, we'll be able to tell if it's him."

"But what's the connection between Cavatelli and the old lady?" Doc asked.

"I don't know. Let's ask her," Smoke responded grimly.

"Smoke, it's after midnight."

Late or not, Smoke wasn't going to waste time waiting around when every minute counted. Sam was missing, and there was no longer a question in his mind that Cavatelli had something to do with that.

"Midnight, seven p.m.—probably the same to her. She's eighty-two." In fact, Smoke didn't recall seeing her outside the apartment building with everyone else. It was entirely possible that she had slept right through the excitement.

Things were quiet when they made it back to the apartment building. The fire and police vehicles were gone, and the residents were safely back inside.

Smoke's repeated knocks on Mrs. Himmelwright's door went unanswered.

The lady from down the hall stuck her head out of her door. "Hey, bud, do you know what time it is?"

"Sorry, ma'am. Just checking on Mrs. Himmelwright. Have you seen her since the fire, by any chance?"

The woman looked at Smoke, Doc, and Church. "You live in 7C," she said, her eyes landing once again on Smoke.

"Yes, ma'am. And I'm concerned because I didn't see Mrs. Himmelwright outside with everyone else. I just want to make sure she's all right."

"Now that you mention it, neither did I. Hang on; let me call the building manager. He can bring up a key."

Smoke wasn't happy about having to wait. He would have preferred to put his lock-picking skills to use once again and be done with it, but a warning look and nod from Church had him saying, "Thanks. I appreciate it."

Fifteen minutes later, the grumbling building manager stepped off the elevator. His knocks, too, went unanswered. When he suggested calling the police before barging in, Smoke took the keys from him and opened the door himself.

He sucked in a breath when the connection between Constance Himmelwright and Anthony Cavatelli instantly became clear.

~ *Sam* ~

Sam came to with a pounding headache. She tried to sit up, but a wave of dizziness and nausea made her close her eyes until the feeling calmed enough that hurling was not a foregone conclusion.

Breathe in slowly. Breathe out slowly. Listen.

The cotton in her mouth seemed to be filling her ears as well, a slight buzzing hum that slowly faded to crackles and pops. When she opened her eyes, her vision slowly cleared until she was able to take in her surroundings. It looked like someone's living room, but an unfamiliar one. The only light came from the fireplace, bathing the space in a warm, flickering glow. It was enough for her to see the bouquets of wildflowers scattered around the room.

Where the hell am I?

"Here, take these. They'll help."

Sam started at the dark figure who suddenly appeared in the doorway, holding out a glass of water in one hand and a couple of pills in the other.

As he closed the distance between them, the evening's events came back to her in a rush.

"Where's Mrs. Himmelwright? What did you do to her?"

The corners of his lips quirked. "Go on; it's okay. Just water and ibuprofen."

What was her elderly neighbor's voice doing, coming out of his mouth?

The last moments in her apartment flashed back to her. Mrs. Himmelwright asking her to call the building manager, then strong arms grabbing her and shoving something over her mouth and nose. Arms that were far too strong to belong to an old woman.

Her head throbbed as she tried to connect the dots. Mrs. Himmelwright wasn't actually an old woman, but a young man with dark, glittering eyes? Could that be right?

"Who are you? What happened? Where are we?"

The man sighed, putting the water and pills down on the side table. "Don't you remember me, Samantha?"

She blinked. The guy knew her name? And he looked hurt that she didn't know his.

Her eyes scanned the room again, looking for something that might lend a clue, but she came up empty. This time, her awakening brain noted the boarded-up windows and old, outdated furnishings. Piles of dirt and debris had been hastily swept toward the corners. Graffiti—some legible, some not—had been spray-painted on walls, where framed paintings still hung.

A living room, yes, but one that hadn't known human occupants for a decade or more.

She looked back at the man before her, knowing with sudden clarity that she was face-to-face with her stalker. A stalker who had quite convincingly pretended to be her elderly neighbor. Had he assumed other personas as well? It was on the tip of her tongue to ask, but her brain overrode the words before she could say them.

Don't antagonize him. Remain calm. Gather

information.

"I'm sorry. My head's a little fuzzy right now. Can you give me a hint?"

He seemed to relax and offered an indulgent smile. "Like a game! Of course. It has been a while, and I suppose I've changed a lot, as have you. I'm no longer that awkward, skinny boy who used to help you unload your grandparents' bakery truck when you came to the resort, and you've grown even more beautiful."

Her mind worked frantically against the lingering fog. The resort he'd mentioned ... he could only be talking about Matt's place. Vague images of a young boy came to mind. Younger than her, he used to run out to meet them at the back entrance. He would stick to her like glue until it was time to leave.

What the hell was his name?

"Anthony?"

His smile was brilliant. "You *do* remember!"

"Of course I do," she said, managing a weak smile, even as her heart pounded and more memories rose to the surface.

Her grandparents hadn't liked him, not at all. In a rare moment of concern, her grandfather had told her that the boy had "the crazy" in his eyes and that she was not to go anywhere with him. At the time, she thought her grandparents were just doing their usual best to squelch anything even remotely fun. Sure, there was something different about Anthony, but he was always nice to her. Then, when she had seen how the staff and guests went out of their way to avoid him, she hadn't had the heart to do the same. Now, it seemed her disobedience and soft heart had come back to bite her in the backside.

Well, there was nothing she could do about that now. Clearly, he was delusional, but she had no idea how far gone he was or what he had in mind. The best things she could do was learn as much as she could, including where they were, and stay alive until an opportunity presented itself or someone found them.

Steve! Steve had been on his way to see her when Mrs. Himmelwright—no, *Anthony*—showed up. How much time had passed since then? Did Steve know she was missing, or did he think she had simply changed her mind?

No, Steve wouldn't think that. He had said he wanted to talk, and she had told him she was making muffins.

The muffins! Had Anthony thought to turn off the oven, or had he left them baking? Had she unintentionally done exactly what the fire chief suspected her of doing and caused a fire that might have hurt people? Hurt Steve?

Sam reined in her panic. Steve was smart. Steve was strong. Steve believed in her. He would know something had happened, that she wouldn't just blow him off. If she couldn't find a way out of this herself, he was her plan B.

Now though, it was time to put plan A into action—make nice with the crazy guy and appeal to his sense of reason.

"It has been a long time. How have you been, Anthony?"

His expression darkened before clearing again. He shrugged. "None of that matters. Now that you and I are together again, things will be better. Do you like the flowers?"

"Yes, the flowers are lovely, thank you."

"I wasn't sure," he said, his dark eyes glistening in the firelight. "You didn't seem to appreciate the others I sent you."

"I didn't know they were from you. You never signed your name."

His lips pursed together, and then he nodded. "Fair enough."

"Anthony, I'd love to catch up with you, but could we do this another time? I don't feel so good. I'd like to go home." Sam didn't think simply asking nicely would work, but it was worth a shot.

"You already are," he said with another grin. "Welcome to your new home, Samantha."

CHAPTER THIRTEEN

~ *Smoke* ~

"Jesus." Smoke stared around the room, shocked by what he saw. Mirrors, costumes, and a huge eight-foot folding table, piled high with makeup, Styrofoam heads with wigs, and an assortment of beards and mustaches.

"Looks like Jim Henson threw up in here," Doc murmured, picking up a familiar curly blue-tinted wig. "Well, I think it's safe to say we found the connection. Gotta say, I didn't see that one coming. How do you want to play this, Smoke?"

Smoke shot a glance at the building manager, who looked like he had just entered *The Twilight Zone*. That made four of them.

"Why don't you take care of calling the cops?" Smoke suggested to the manager.

"Yeah, yeah. Good idea. Uh, what should I tell them?"

"Tell them the truth. You received a call from a concerned resident and came up to check on Mrs. Himmelwright."

"Right."

"Probably best to call from your office. Don't want to touch anything that might be evidence."

"Yeah, evidence. Good point. What about you guys?"

"No need to mention us. We were just here to provide backup in case you needed it."

The building manager pulled his eyes away from the costumes and props to look at the three men surrounding him. Realization dawned in his eyes. "Hey, are you guys special ops or something?"

"Or something," Church said vaguely.

"I knew it! Well, you can count on me." He stood taller. "Private David Yocum, National Guard, at your service."

"At ease, Private," Church said, his voice commanding and authoritative. "Five minutes is all we need."

"Yes, sir. Understood, sir."

Doc smiled after the building manager left. "Laid it on a bit thick there, didn't you, *sir*?"

Church's lips quirked. "Okay, let's do a quick sweep and see what this crazy bastard left for us to find."

Smoke wasted no time. The layout was exactly the same as his apartment. He headed for the bedroom, his stomach roiling when he flipped on the light and saw the walls plastered with pictures of Sam. Sam at the coffee shop. Sam stepping out of the apartment building. Sam on her balcony, sipping tea.

Forcing the panic down, he looked for something, anything that might provide a clue as to where he had taken her, but found nothing. Doc and Church hadn't had much luck either.

Church's phone chimed, breaking the silence.

"It's Cage." He raised it up to his ear and listened. "Got it. On our way."

"Tell me something good," Smoke said.

"Cage's buddy came through. He thinks he knows where we can find Cavatelli."

Thank God.

Smoke was certain that when they found Cavatelli, they would find Sam. Cavatelli's future was bleak at best, but if even one hair on Sam's head had been harmed, Cavatelli was going to experience firsthand the extreme prejudice of a pissed-off Navy SEAL.

"He's mine."

They made plans to meet up at Sanctuary in thirty minutes. After a brief stop at Smoke's apartment to pick up some of his favorite toys, they were on the road.

He wasn't the only one who had grabbed some gear. By the time they made it to the trailer, the others were already there, dressed in tactical gear, armed and ready.

"Sounds like little Anthony is even more fucked up than we thought," Heff said after reading the reports Cage had forwarded to them. "Being a pyro is just the tip of the iceberg. He's a delusional psychopath, too."

"How the hell did they let this guy out?" Mad Dog mused.

"He's a delusional psycho, but apparently, an accomplished actor as well," Doc told them. "You should have seen his place. The guy must have had two dozen different identities. Convincing a couple of overworked docs he had his shit under control would've been a simple matter."

"Add in an overcrowded, underfunded state facility, and they were probably only too happy to believe he'd changed and showed him the door."

Smoke's skin felt tight, and his adrenaline was pumping. They needed to *go*. "So, where is he now?" he asked impatiently.

"Cavatelli's early years were spent with his mom in a small mining town about a hundred miles northwest of here. The town's abandoned now. Everyone was evacuated when they discovered the underground mines were on fire and there was no way to put them out. My buddy turned a couple of satellites that way, and there are signs of possible activity up there."

"Holy shit, your guy can control satellites? I thought he was a civilian."

"I never said that," Cage said. "But technically, he is now, I guess. He was an active-duty SEAL at one time."

"Might just be kids or thrill seekers up there,"

Heff interjected.

"Maybe, but it's the best lead we have right now."

"Then, what are we waiting for?" Anxious to get out of the cramped quarters and be on their way, Smoke pushed open the door and pointed his boots in the direction of the vehicles.

"Smoke." Church stepped in front of him. "I know this is personal for you, man. I need to know where your head's at."

Resisting the urge to move him out of the way, Smoke reminded himself that Church had been their team leader. "My head is just fine. And I could ask you the same thing. You've got history with Cavatelli, too."

A muscle twitched in Church's jaw. "Point taken. Let's go get Sam and take care of this son of a bitch once and for all."

~ Sam ~

"Aren't they beautiful?" Anthony asked, sweeping his hand toward the fireplace.

He sat on the sofa beside her, close, but not uncomfortably so. Half of the ham and cheese hoagie he had brought for them to share remained untouched on the TV tray table in front of her.

"The way they dance like that, it's mesmerizing. *I* make them dance. They're dancing for you, you know. They're happy for us. You should eat."

He was nuts. Certifiably insane. He stayed calm though as long as she didn't do or say anything to upset him.

"Don't worry, Samantha; you're safe here. I'll take care of you. No one will bother us."

"No one?" she asked. They were in a boarded-up house, so maybe there were other houses around, too. Chances for help. "What about neighbors?"

He chuckled, his eyes glistening again. "Gone. They're all gone."

Oh God. The sips of water she had forced down threatened to make a dramatic reappearance. "Did you …"

It took a moment for him to grasp what she was asking. When he did, his eyes widened. "No, of course not. But I suppose, in a way, I am responsible."

"I don't understand."

"No, I can see that," he said, leaning forward, as if to share a great secret. "This town was once called Miner's Hollow. It's abandoned now."

Miner's Hollow. She had heard of the town. It had made national news years earlier, right about the time she went to live with her grandparents. It was a mountain town, known for its rich veins of anthracite coal. The actual mines had closed down a long time ago, well before the underground fires, but the tunnels remained. Somehow, a fire started down there. By the time it had been discovered, it had spread too far, resisting any and all attempts to contain it.

Experts said that with the nearly inexhaustible fuel supply, it could take more than a hundred years to burn itself out and would become increasingly hazardous to the residents. As a result, the government paid pennies on the dollar to buy up the properties and forcibly evacuate everyone within a fifty-mile radius. Roads had been closed and bridges destroyed to discourage the curious from poking around.

Sam's hopes faded. If they were in Miner's Hollow, it was unlikely anyone would find them.

"I didn't start the fires intentionally," Anthony said. "Well, I mean, I *did*"—he grinned shyly—"but I never imagined the possibilities. I hated this town, hated everyone in it. My mother grew up here, but you wouldn't know it by the way they treated her. Treated *me*. I'm glad they're gone. Now, we have the whole place to ourselves."

"I remember seeing pictures on TV," Sam said, her mind whirling. "Smoke coming up through cracks in the ground, the nearby forests glowing red at night. Like hell on earth, they called it."

His expression grew stormy, and he clenched his fists. "No, Samantha, *hell* is living in a world where people don't understand you. Where they hate you because you're special." Just as suddenly, his face cleared. "But not you, Samantha. You *saw* me. And now, we can be happy together."

"We can't stay here, Anthony," she said, striving to keep her voice calm and rational, even as the panic tried to gain hold. "There's no electricity, no heat."

"The fire will provide," he said confidently. "You and I, we're going to live a simpler life. We can grow our own vegetables. Did you know that mixing ash and dirt creates an ideal garden bed? And I'll hunt for us. There's plenty of game in the woods now that the people are gone, and I'm an excellent shot. We can roast fresh meat on a spit, just like they did in the old days." His eyes lit up with the possibilities. "Mountain-fed spring water, too. Best you've ever tasted."

"I'm afraid I don't know much about surviving in the wilderness."

He patted her arm; she fought not to recoil. "Don't worry, Samantha; I'll teach you everything you need to know. We'll be like pioneers!"

"But surely, we'll be missed," Sam said weakly. "Someone will come looking for us." *God, please let someone come look for us.*

"Don't you worry, Samantha. I've taken care of everything."

The certainty in his voice was chilling.

"What do you mean, Anthony? What have you taken care of?"

"Everyone who tried to keep us apart is gone now. Your grandparents, Mr. Santori, that guy who wouldn't leave you alone."

Oh God. "The fires. It was you."

He nodded. "I did it for you, Samantha. For us. Just like those people at the resort who were going to make my mom and me leave. And your grandparents, they wouldn't tell me where you were. Mr. Santori hurt you when he cheated you like that. He had to pay."

Sam felt as if her entire world had tilted on its axis. "And Steve?"

Anthony grinned. "I made a little adjustment to his brakes—that's all. The fire in the apartment building though? That was all you."

CHAPTER FOURTEEN

~ *Smoke* ~

Working together felt comfortable, familiar. This was his team. Some of them, he had trusted them with his life more times than he could count. Now, he was trusting them with Sam's.

They had all agreed that involving the local authorities wasn't in their best interests. Not only did Smoke have an open warrant out for his arrest, but it would take too long to explain everything. And since they couldn't explain where or how they had gotten their information, the chances of being believed hovered between slim and none.

That was fine by him. Smoke didn't have a very high opinion of the ones he'd dealt with thus far, and Church seemed to agree. Spend a lot of time with someone, and you learned to read them. Smoke was certain Church knew a lot more about the Sumneyville authorities than he was letting on.

For now, they were operating on their own with clear goals—rescue Sam and eliminate any further threat.

They drove as far as they dared, using

unmarked access roads and GPS coordinates. Dressed in black and prepared for any eventuality, they covered the rest of the way on foot.

Miner's Hollow was a ghost town. What had once been neighborhoods now looked like a postapocalyptic war zone. Homes sat abandoned. Weeds and scrub pushed up through cracks in once-smooth roads and sidewalks. The only source of light beyond the waning crescent moon were areas of indistinct red glow along the ground—an indication of the slow-burning anthracite veins below the surface. Occasional tendrils of smoke drifted just above the ground, adding to the spooky feel.

Night vision goggles and years of stealth experience brought them to the childhood home of Anthony Cavatelli. The house was an unpretentious, boxy thing, wedged between two others that looked just like it. The windows were boarded up and faded *No Trespassing* signs were posted on the doors.

At first glance, they saw nothing unusual.

Then, Heff's whisper came through their earpieces. "Do you smell that?"

Smoke lifted his nose and sniffed. Smoke. But not the same scent that permeated the whole area. This wasn't the scent of an underground fire. This was the scent of wood smoke.

With a series of hand signals, Church directed them into positions surrounding the home. When everyone was in place, another predetermined signal closed their circle.

Suddenly, a discordant series of metallic clanks rang out, breaking the eerie silence.

"Fuck," muttered Mad Dog into the comm sets. "Trip wire."

~ *Sam* ~

"What was that?" Sam asked, startled by the sudden clanging noise. It sounded as if someone had just dumped a bunch of aluminum cans outside the door.

Anthony shot to his feet, his good mood evaporating instantly. "The alarm. Come. We have to go."

"Go where?" Sam asked as Anthony yanked her to her feet and practically dragged her toward an interior door. She struggled and tried to hold back, but he was too strong.

"Hurry!" he prodded.

He shut the door behind them and shot ahead of her, pulling her down the stairs. She slipped in the darkness partway down, causing them both to tumble the rest of the way. Anthony got the worst of it, grunting as she landed on top of him.

She scrabbled to her feet with the intention of running back up the steps, but he grabbed her ankle and pulled her back down.

"No!" he hissed. "This way!"

"Anthony, stop!" she cried, hoping whoever had tripped Anthony's alarm would hear her.

"Shh!" he commanded.

He covered her mouth with one hand and curled his other arm around her waist. Pulling her tightly against his body, he then dragged her backward, away from the steps and back against the wall.

They stood in silence, listening, her heart pounding against the inside of her ribs. Then, she heard it. The creak of a floorboard directly above their heads.

Knowing this might be her only chance, Sam lifted her foot and stomped hard on Anthony's instep. She followed that up by immediately bending at the waist and shoving her elbow backward with a sharp jab into his solar plexus.

He grunted again but didn't let go. Instead, he grabbed her by the hair and spun them both around, slamming her back up against the concrete wall.

"I won't let them take you from me," he vowed as he pressed his body against hers. "You are mine, and we are going to be happy together. I'm sorry about this, Samantha. I know you don't understand yet, but it's for the best."

She barely had time to register his words before pain exploded against the side of her face, and then everything went dark.

~ *Smoke* ~

"In my sights."

Smoke had heard Heff speak those words a hundred times before, but they had never sounded sweeter.

"Copy that. Can you get a lock?"

"Negative. He's running, got Sam in a fireman's carry, heading east."

"Slow his roll, Mad Dog."

"On it."

Smoke emerged through the now-open double bulkhead doors leading from the basement into the side yard, just in time to see Cavatelli slip through the overgrown hedgerow separating the properties. He put on a burst of speed and followed, emerging on the other side, then hitting the ground when he caught the glint of steel. The shot missed him, but it was close enough for him to feel the breeze.

"Fucker's got a gun," Smoke said, getting to his feet and following.

"So do we," commented Cage. "And ours are bigger."

Anthony might have thought he had an advantage by knowing the area, but that wasn't going to save him. He had no idea who he was up against or the lengths they would go to, to get Sam back, safe and sound. Sam was Smoke's and, therefore, theirs.

"Let the girl go," Church said from just ahead.

Smoke drew closer to find Anthony cornered in a detached garage by both Mad Dog and Church.

The situation was tense. Cavatelli had Sam held in front of him like a shield, the gun moving back and forth between Mad Dog and Church. Sam's head and limbs hung limp, as if she was unconscious. The air was thick with the pungent smell of gasoline.

"Never. She's mine."

"Let me hear her say that."

"Stay back!"

"Can't do that, Anthony."

"How do you know my name?"

"We know everything, Anthony. We know about the fires. We know how you've been terrorizing Sam."

"No! I love her. It was all for her."

"It's over, Anthony. Put down the gun before someone gets hurt."

Smoke had seen his share of men come to the realization they couldn't win. They all reacted the same. The moment of desperation in their eyes, followed by blind rage, and finally, resignation and acceptance. Anthony was no different.

Except none of those men had been holding his woman when the truth sank in.

"If you know everything," Anthony said, his voice oddly hollow, "then you know how this is going to end."

A snick sounded in the silence as the hand

around Sam's waist moved, sparking a lighter to flame. The smile on the sick bastard's face was pure madness as he tossed the lighter onto the floor … *the floor drenched with gasoline.*

Several things happened in quick succession. Smoke charged forward, intent on getting Sam away from the flames. Anthony squeezed off two quick shots, even as Heff took his one. Fire flared to life, filling the space within seconds.

Smoke barely registered the burn in his shoulder. All he could see was Sam falling toward the fuel-drenched floor. A sudden, sharp pain in his leg caused him to stumble. Regardless, he dove forward, covering Sam with his own body to keep the flames away, and rolled. Church and Mad Dog were there a heartbeat later, dragging them both to safety.

"Check her out first," Smoke commanded when Doc started poking at him.

Doc didn't argue, turning his attention to Sam and giving her a quick once-over. "Strong heartbeat, good breathing, pupils responsive."

"She's okay?"

"Yeah, Smoke, she's okay. She's going to have a hell of a headache and a nice shiner when she wakes up, but that's it. Mind if I take a look at your bullet wounds now?"

"Knock yourself out."

~ *Sam* ~

Sam came to with another headache. This one was different than the last one. It came less from inside her head and more from the aching throb along the side of her face.

Sensing movement, she opened her eyes and lifted her head. It was dark, and she was lying on something firm and warm. No, not some*thing*. Some*one*. Someone with a large hand, who was gently stroking her hair. Someone who smelled like …

"Steve?"

"Yeah, baby," he said, his voice somewhat groggy. "I got you."

Baby?

She lifted her head from his shoulder, afraid she was dreaming. But she wasn't dreaming. She was in the backseat of an SUV, tucked up against Steve's warm, hard body. In the muted lights of the dashboard, she could see his handsome face, see his beautiful eyes as he gave her a tired but very real smile.

"Hey, Sam," Church greeted, meeting her eyes in the rearview mirror. He was driving, and Doc was sitting in the front passenger seat.

"You found me."

"Always," Steve said.

"But how?"

"Long story."

"Anthony?"

"Is no longer an issue."

A sense of relief flooded her, but it was short-lived.

"Why does it look like there are bloody bandages on your shoulder and leg?"

"Because somebody got his ass shot," Church grunted out.

"It's all good," Steve said in a calming tone, though he directed an irritated glance toward the front.

"Good? How can it be *good*? You were *shot*."

He grinned at her as if he weren't sporting fresh, bleeding bullet wounds. "You're beautiful, you know that?"

Sam turned toward Doc. "You gave him drugs, didn't you?"

"Had to. He was whining like a baby."

"Was not," Steve said, giving him a lethargic middle-finger salute. "At least I'm not the one who got tripped up by a string of twenty-year-old beer cans."

"That wasn't me. That was Mad Dog."

"Not what he said."

Sam couldn't believe they were joking about this. She was just about to say something when Steve tugged her closer, using the arm that *hadn't* been shot.

"Later, okay, Sam?" he said quietly.

"Okay," she agreed, hearing the pain in his

voice beneath the teasing. She would get answers, but at that moment, all she wanted to do was feel him next to her, solid and breathing and real.

CHAPTER FIFTEEN

~ *Smoke* ~

The shot Doc had given him once they got in the vehicle was making it hard to keep his eyes open, but he wanted to reassure Sam that he was fine. He had seen the fear in her eyes, felt her trembling against him. He'd meant what he said. He would explain everything, but later—once Doc patched him up and they were far away from Miner's Hollow.

None of them knew if the fire would be spotted or if crews would be sent out, but Cage's friend had warned about drones that did routine sweeps, trying to catch kids and others who snuck into the restricted area. In any case, it was better if their presence and involvement in the evening's events were kept strictly between them.

Church pulled the vehicle into a parking garage. Mad Dog, Heff, and Cage were already there, waiting.

"Express elevator, at your service." Heff grinned with an exaggerated bow.

"Wait, this isn't a hospital? Why aren't we

going to a hospital? Steve was *shot*."

"Hospitals have to report gunshot wounds," Church told her simply. "And tonight never happened."

Sam's eyes widened, and her bottom lip trembled.

"He's going to be fine, Sam," Doc said gently. "I promise."

"I'm going to hold you to that."

"You and Smoke need to lie low for a couple of days, so we've booked a suite," Church told her. "We'll grab whatever you need and bring it to you. Room service is okay, but if you need anything else, one of us will provide it. Got it?"

"Got it." She nodded, then slipped her arm around Steve's waist. "Well, what are we waiting for? This man needs rest."

Smoke smiled at the firmness of her tone, then concentrated on staying upright long enough to make it into the hotel room.

The next few hours passed in a blur. Doc removed the bullet from his shoulder. The one he had taken in the thigh had gone right through.

Smoke vaguely remembered Sam cleaning him up with a warm washcloth, then stretching beside him on the king-size bed. When he woke up again, he was in bed alone. Sam emerged from the bathroom, a cloud of steam billowing out behind her.

"Hey," she said softly, smiling at him. "You're

awake. How do you feel?"

"Like I was shot a few times," he joked.

The light in her eyes faded, her lips turning downward at the corners. He would have to remember not to joke about that.

"Come here."

She did, taking tiny, tentative steps.

"Sit, please." He patted the bed beside him.

When she sat down gently on the edge of the bed, he lifted his good arm and stroked tenderly over the left side of her face, where a dark purple bruise was already forming. "I'm sorry I didn't get there sooner."

Her eyes softened and filled with tears. "I'm just glad you came."

He pulled her close. "I'll always come for you, Sam. Always."

The events of the last few days finally caught up to her, and she broke down. Smoke held her in his arms while she sobbed, then continued to hold her when she finally fell into an exhausted sleep.

~ *Sam* ~

Sam paused in the doorway, taking a moment to enjoy the view. The bathroom door was open, and Steve was shaving. A white towel was slung low over his lean hips, revealing a lovely, masculine terrain of ridges and valleys, hard curves, and stark angles. His dark hair was shaggy, towel-dried but uncombed. She licked her lips as he lifted his chin and drew the razor upward in smooth, practiced strokes.

Other than the small waterproof patch on his shoulder, there was no other visible indication that he had been shot only a few days earlier.

"See something you like, Sam?"

His deep voice drew her eyes upward to meet his in the mirror. While she had been ogling, he had finished and was now drying his smooth, clean-shaven jaw with a hand towel.

Heat rushed into her cheeks, but she held her ground. "Maybe."

He grinned, and just like that, the blossoming heat between her legs flared.

"I just came to see if you were hungry," she said, wishing she hadn't sounded so breathless.

He turned just enough to drop his gaze in a slow, suggestive perusal, then back up to meet her eyes. "Yeah, I could eat."

That slow burn, the same one that had been growing over the last few days, flared once again.

He had asked her to stay with him each night, saying he slept better, knowing she was nearby. Considering the man had gotten shot *twice* while rescuing her, it was the least she could do.

Not that she didn't want to. She slept better, too, knowing he was right there.

Their cuddling thus far had been done clothed

and PG-rated. She didn't count the time she had woken up with his palm cupping her ass or the stiff, large part of him that had poked her backside when she snuggled against him. He had been asleep those times, and it wasn't as if she'd minded. Just as she hoped he wouldn't have minded had he woken up to find her arm wrapped around him and her thigh hitched up over his hip.

But now ... now, they were both awake, and there was no mistaking the blatant desire in his eyes.

Just like that, her nipples pebbled beneath the thin cotton tee, hard enough to make themselves known. His eyes flicked down, lingered for a moment, then back up again. Her eyes flicked downward, too, but at her angle, she couldn't tell if he was in the midst of experiencing a similar reaction.

Part of her urged her to move forward and find out, preferably on her knees. Another part warned against it. Not because she thought he would refuse, but because she didn't want to become more attached to him than she already was. It had hit her that first night as she remained awake—watching over him as he slept under the powerful painkillers, ones he had needed because of her—that somewhere along the line, she had started falling in love with him.

"Well," she said, clearing her throat softly, "I'll go and order us something."

She turned, but before she could take two steps, he was there, his hands on her upper arms, his heat at her back.

"Sam."

She closed her eyes, soaking in the moment. "Yes?"

"Look at me."

She didn't want to. If he looked in her eyes now, he would see everything.

With strong hands, he gently coaxed her around to face him. "Sam. Open those pretty eyes and look at me."

She did.

His gaze was so intense. Questioning. And there was something else there that she hadn't seen before—uncertainty. Could he possibly be feeling the same things she was?

"I want you, Sam."

"I want you, too." She whispered the words. "But …"

"No buts," he told her, bringing his hands up to cup her face. "Not tonight. I almost lost you. I almost lost you before I …"

"Before you what?"

"Before I had a chance to do this." Steve lowered his head and brushed his lips over hers once, twice, before pressing more firmly.

Just that quickly, any resistance she'd had melted away along with the rest of the world.

She kissed him back, parting her lips to taste

him. He groaned softly in the back of his throat, pulling her closer and eliminating any doubts she might have had about him being as aroused as she was.

She moved her hand between them, tugging on the towel to release him. He made another sound—this one a warning growl. She registered it, then ignored it, encircling his hard length and moving up and down, imagining what that would feel like inside of her. Velvety smooth and hot, textured just enough for maximum pleasure. Broad head, thick root, and—she reached between his legs and cupped him—full and tight.

This man was perfect. And those erotic fantasies she had privately entertained? They didn't hold a candle to the real thing.

"*Sam.*"

A shiver of feminine pleasure ran through her at the husky tone of his voice. *She* had done that.

Tomorrow no longer mattered. He wanted her right here, right now, just as much as she wanted him.

She ran her thumb over the wet tip, her mouth watering for a taste. Then, before she lost her nerve, she went down on her knees and gave him an open-mouthed kiss.

"Fuck, Sam." Those large hands burrowed into her hair.

For a moment, she thought he was going to attempt to pull her away, but then he curled his fingers and held on, the slight pull ramping up her own desire.

She licked, she tongued, she sucked and fondled, using the sounds he made and the way his muscles tensed to guide her.

"Sam, baby, you have to stop."

"Why?"

"Because I want the first time to be inside you."

The *first* time, suggesting there would be others. She liked the sound of that.

Releasing him, she kissed her way over his hip, along his abs, detouring slightly to tongue each nipple before meeting his lips again.

"Bed. Now."

She grinned, the realization that she had reduced him to single-worded commands a heady one.

In her fantasies, she had allowed him to undress her, but she was too revved up for that now. One step, and she was lifting her top over her head. At the fourth step, her thumbs hooked into the waistband of her yoga pants and pushed downward, allowing her to walk right out of them. By the time she reached the bed, she was naked, her clothes like a trail of breadcrumbs behind her.

Before she could turn, a large palm landed on her flank, not painful, but erotic.

"Your turn," he said.

"No," she refuted when he started to get on his

knees. "It'll be better for your leg if you lie down."

He grinned wolfishly and spread himself out on the bed, a feast for her eyes. "Come over here, woman, and straddle my face."

The pure carnality of his words ratcheted her arousal another notch. This was a new experience for her. She had always been too shy, too embarrassed to allow such a thing. But with Steve, self-consciousness took a backseat to need. She wanted to feel his lips between her legs. She wanted to feel his tongue gliding along her slick folds.

He gripped her hips, looking at her with reverence. Surely, he could see how wet she was for him. How she ached.

"So pretty," he crooned, guiding her closer.

The first touch of his tongue was gentle yet enough to make her cry out. The second even better. The man had skills, flattening his tongue one moment, then spearing her the next. It felt amazing, so amazing that her hips started moving right along with him.

Soon, a thick finger circled her entrance, teasing and stretching before gliding inside. He moved it in and out several times, bringing her to the brink. Then, he wrapped those firm male lips around the current center of her sensory universe and sucked. She shattered, losing herself in a maelstrom of feeling until her body shook.

"You're stunning when you come," he told her. "I need to see it again."

She opened her eyes and looked down to find him with the smug expression of a man who knew he had done an exemplary job. There was something else in his eyes, too. Something warm that would have made her go all gooey inside if she hadn't already melted.

As anxious as she was to feel him inside her, they had to be careful—for both their sakes.

Apparently, he was thinking along the same lines because he said, "Check the bag."

She left the bed only long enough to open the zippered black duffel and peer inside. Her eyes grew wide when she pulled out an entire box of condoms. In bright, bold letters, the label proclaimed, *For Her Pleasure Variety Pack*. She held them up for Steve to see.

"Fucking Heff," he said on a chuckle. "But right now, I'm thankful for his foresight. Come back up here, woman, and keep that box in reach."

His injuries meant they had to get creative, but Sam would have dangled from the ceiling to have this man if she had to. Thankfully, it didn't come to that, and with a few mindful choices, she got her wish.

She sank onto him, working her way downward in little increments until he was seated fully inside her.

"A perfect fit," he murmured, his body tense with desire.

Sam had to agree.

She rode him slowly, savoring each moment, rocking her hips and squeezing, taking him with her as they climbed new heights. Making love with him was unlike anything she had ever experienced. She had never felt as close to anyone as she did in those moments. There was passion, yes, but it went far beyond a physical thing. When Steve was inside her, she felt him in her heart and soul as much as her body.

All too soon, they reached their peaks, and looking into each other's eyes, they stepped off the edge together.

"That was incredible," he said as he pulled her close, holding her through the aftershocks.

It *was* incredible. The best experience she had ever had. So, why did part of her feel like crying?

"Okay, *now*, I'm hungry," he teased.

"I'll order something, but it may take a while."

He grinned. "Totally worth it."

Was it? she wondered. Because now, she wasn't sure they could go back to just being friends.

And watching him walk away would hurt even more.

CHAPTER SIXTEEN

~ *Sam* ~

Sam knew their idyllic time together was coming to an end when Church and Cage came by and told them everything had been taken care of. The fire in Miner's Hollow had been discovered and contained, but not before it had ravaged at least half the houses on the block. According to official reports, the fire had been blamed as a suicide attempt of an unidentified person, the only known victim of the blaze.

Anthony was dead, killed by his precious fire.

Sam asked Cage to let her read the file he'd created on Anthony before he destroyed it.

Anthony's early years hadn't been easy. When his mom had gotten pregnant at the age of fifteen, her parents hadn't handled it well and made life hell for her and Anthony until she finally saved up enough money from working odd jobs to move away. Some of the doctors at the facility where he had been placed later theorized that abuse by his grandfather might have altered an otherwise highly intelligent boy.

Despite everything, she couldn't help feeling a little sorry for the man he might have been under different circumstances. Living with misunderstood mental illness was something Sam was familiar with. Her mother had battled a severe bipolar disorder and hadn't gotten the treatment she needed because Sam's grandparents had refused to recognize it as a "real" problem until it was too late. Something else her mother and Anthony had in common—they had both died at their own hands when they couldn't see another way out.

The formal charges against Steve had been dropped after a few discreet phone calls. A thorough inspection proved that his brake lines had been tampered with, negating claims that he had deliberately and willfully led police on a high-speed car chase, endangering the lives of the officers and innocent civilians in the process.

Subduing two local cops and absconding with their cruiser was more difficult to explain away, but somehow, those charges were dropped, too. Officers Joe and Lenny reportedly hadn't been too happy about it, but the directive had come from pretty high up.

Sam didn't ask too many questions, figuring men who had been SEALs for as long as they had, had earned a few markers to cash in when the need arose.

Cage had already managed to exonerate her for the fire at the coffee shop by obtaining security camera footage from one of the adjacent businesses—something the police should have done. The video clearly showed an "unidentified male" breaking into the back entrance of the shop and leaving again moments before the fire.

Neither Chief Freed nor Chief Petraski seemed pleased by that. Sam had a feeling they would much rather have continued to cast suspicion her way. Well, that was too bad for them. She hadn't done anything wrong, and she refused to be bullied by them or their small-town, small-minded mentality.

She did ask about Mr. Santori. Despite everything that had happened, she felt a pang of sympathy for him. Cage assured her that as soon as the official investigation wrapped up, the old man would be collecting a tidy sum in insurance money and have no trouble moving forward with his retirement plans.

Dealing with the oven fire at the apartment complex was a bit trickier. According to Church, both the fire chief and the police chief wanted to question Sam about the fire and her whereabouts that night. Steve wasn't happy about that. He wanted Cage to do something, but she told him she wanted to handle it on her own.

She couldn't tell them the truth about everything that had happened that night, not without raising even more questions and prompting an official investigation. That would mean revealing the parts Steve, Church, and the rest of them had played, and she wasn't going to do that, not when they had gone to such lengths for her.

In the end, the apartment fire had been ruled an accident, and charges were not filed. She'd agreed to give up her security deposit to pay for a professional service to come in and clean up the damage caused by smoke and the use of fire extinguishers.

With everything taken care of, reality crashed back into her life with a vengeance. She was unemployed, homeless, and her nest egg was dwindling quickly.

As wonderful as her time with Steve had been, it couldn't last forever. She had known that and had been trying to prepare herself. She had to salvage what she could and move on. She wasn't sure where she was going to go; she just knew there wasn't much left in Sumneyville for her any longer. Her dreams of owning the coffee shop were gone, and while she had officially been cleared of any wrongdoing, the people there would always look upon her with suspicion.

She and Steve hadn't talked about what would happen next. They hadn't really talked about much of anything. He, like she, seemed content to make the most of the time they had together in other ways.

Their futures couldn't have been more different. He had a job and a place waiting for him. She overheard Church tell him that they had been working double time on getting a cabin habitable for him at the resort and it was almost finished. Sam was happy for him. She really was. He had his team and a purpose. He was a good man, and he deserved nothing less.

Her? Well, she would do what she always did. She would find a way to deal with what life handed her and move on. This wasn't the first time in her life things hadn't gone according to plan and she had to start over. She just had to think positively and look at it as an opportunity to move forward. When one door closed, another opened, right?

Leaving Steve and Church to talk, she made a cup of tea and went into the bedroom to pack.

~ Smoke ~

"What's up with Sam?" Church asked once the bedroom door closed behind her. "She's not happy with the offer?"

Smoke shook his head. "I haven't told her yet."

Church lifted a brow. "Why the hell not?"

"I don't know."

"Bullshit."

Church was right. It *was* bullshit. Smoke knew exactly why he hadn't said anything to Sam about Church's idea for her to move up to the resort—because he wasn't sure she would say yes.

He didn't know how she would feel about

moving in with him. Sure, the last few days had been amazing, but just because *he* was ready for the next step didn't mean *she* was.

He'd always gone with his gut, and lately, it had been screaming for him to grab her with both hands and never let go. She made him feel things no other woman ever had, and when he thought about what might have happened if they hadn't found her in time … well, he didn't like to think about that.

The thing was, he wasn't the easiest guy to get along with. He was still dealing with his demons, though admittedly, that wasn't as hard to do with Sam around. When he had woken up in the grips of a panic attack a few nights earlier, he'd found her stroking his back and whispering calming words, bringing him back to reality.

It wasn't like he had much to offer her either. Asking her to move into a cabin with him wasn't exactly wine and roses. They wouldn't have a lot of luxuries, and the next year or so would be a lot of hard work. Even the promise of giving her free rein over the new kitchen and eating area to create her own place might not be enough.

"If you don't ask her, I will," Church told him. "The guys are already threatening to stage a protest if she doesn't come on board."

Smoke's lips quirked. There were those blurred lines and crossed boundaries coming back to bite him in the ass again. This time though, he didn't mind so much.

"They'd choose her over me?"

"In a red-hot minute," Church told him with a quirk of his own. "Of course, the ideal is to have you both on the team, *if* you can take your balls out of your purse long enough to convince her of that. And if you can't handle the job, Heff's offered to—"

"*The hell he will!*"

Church gave him a rare but genuine smile. "Yeah, I thought so. Seriously, Smoke, what gives? You two are the real deal, man. You'd be an idiot to let her walk away."

"I know. But it's a lot to ask."

"I take it back. You *are* an idiot. The way she looks at you? She'd follow you to the ends of the earth if you asked her to."

"You think?"

"No question. But she's not the kind of woman who'd do so blindly. She needs to know you want her there. Do you?"

"The truth? I can't imagine my life without her."

"Then, what the hell are you waiting for?" Church stood up. "Go talk to your woman. Do what you gotta do—*beg* if you have to—but *don't* let her walk away. We'll be waiting on you. *Both* of you."

Was Church right? Would Sam be willing to follow him—or better yet, walk beside him—into the next chapter?

Well, there was only one way to find out.

Smoke stalked to the bedroom door and took a deep, fortifying breath. He could do this. He was a SEAL. And more importantly, he was a man who had found his *one*.

"Come in," Sam called out after he knocked.

He pushed the door open to find her sitting on the edge of the bed, a packed bag beside her, her expression unreadable.

"Is it time to go?"

"Yeah, just about. But there's something I want to talk to you about first."

Something like pain flashed in her pretty eyes, but it was gone before he could be sure. Some of his confidence faltered. Did she know what he was going to say?

"It's okay, Steve."

"What is?"

She shrugged, picking at a nonexistent piece of something on her jeans. "I understand."

He blinked in confusion. "What do you understand?"

"That it's been great, but it's time to move on."

She summoned a weak smile, but he wasn't fooled. She wasn't any happier about leaving than he was.

Deep in his chest, his heart thudded with hope, and his confidence surged. If she dared to look him in the eyes, she might see them glistening.

"Yes, it is," he agreed.

She winced slightly, and his heart soared.

"Your friends are counting on you, and they're a great bunch of guys."

"Yes, they are."

"Church's vision is going to be a success. I know it is."

"Yes, it will."

With each ready agreement, her frown intensified. He could barely contain his glee.

Finally, he decided he'd let her go on long enough. "That's what I want to talk to you about. See, Church—well, all of us really—decided that we need the kitchen up and running as soon as possible. And we agree that you are the best person for the job."

Her eyes lifted. "Seriously?"

"Seriously. They've been suffering withdrawals, forced to rely on mini-mart coffee and mass-produced pastries. It's been awful."

"I bet," she murmured.

"And with your business experience, you're the perfect choice. None of us know the first thing about running a restaurant, and it's one less thing for Church to worry about. He could hire from the outside, but he likes to keep things close and personal, you know? And he already considers you part of the team."

"*He* does?" Her eyes filled with surprise.

"Yep. There is the issue of housing though. You might have noticed that on-site accommodations are in short supply." When her burgeoning smile faded a little, he was quick to add, "That's why you should move in with me."

"What?"

He almost smiled at how large her eyes became, but he was afraid she might misinterpret it and think he wasn't one hundred percent serious.

"Yeah. Church told me this morning that they've managed to make one of the cabins habitable. It's nothing like this"—he waved his arm around the hotel room—"but it has working plumbing and electricity. Of course, the downside is, you'd be stuck with me for the foreseeable future. Do you think you can handle that?"

"That depends," she said slowly.

"On what?"

"On how *you* feel about that."

"Oh, well, that's a no-brainer for me. I've already told Church that it's a package deal. If you're not coming, I'm not coming."

Her eyes grew even larger. "Why would you do that?"

"Because I'm falling in love with you, Sam. Did I forget to mention that?"

She blinked. "Yes. You did."

"Oh. Well, I am. Listen, Sam, I realize this is a big step, maybe one you're not ready for, but—"

"Yes." Tears welled in her eyes, but he pushed forward, needing her to understand how serious he was.

"I think we can make this work. I … wait.

What did you say?"

Her expression softened, and she smiled at him. "I said yes, Steve."

"Yes to what part?" he asked cautiously. He wanted to be absolutely one hundred percent certain she was saying what he hoped she was saying.

"All of it," she said, rising to slip her arms around his waist. "Yes to the job. Yes to the cabin. Yes to you."

Relief flooded through him. He lowered his head and branded her with a soul-searing kiss. "Yeah?"

"Yeah. Think you can handle that?"

"Baby, I'm a SEAL. And with you by my side, I can handle anything."

EPILOGUE
SIX MONTHS LATER

~ *Sam* ~

The weather had turned colder. The brilliance of autumn was fading, but the mountains were still awash with color. In the newly renovated dining area, the tinted floor-to-ceiling glass panels between thick columns overlooked it all—from stunning sunrises on the east to the spectacular sunsets on the west.

Sam walked around the space with a critical eye, adjusting a plant here, straightening a saltshaker there. The decor was open and airy, comfortable, but not overdone. Tables were easily moveable to accommodate single guests or bigger groups.

Steve slipped his arms around her waist. "Stop worrying. It looks amazing."

She leaned back into his hard body, welcoming the rush of warmth she always felt when he held her like this.

It had been six months since she had moved out

here with him, and each day was better than the last. It wasn't all easy though. They had worked long and hard alongside the other members of the team to get things ready for their first guests.

As promised, Church had given Sam free rein over the kitchens and common dining space. The result was an operation capable of turning out top-quality meals in a casual, relaxed setting.

She turned in his arms. "I hope so."

The first guests were due to arrive tomorrow.

"They'll love it," he said with enough confidence that she almost believed it. "But there's something we have to take care of before they arrive."

"Oh?" she asked, her mind desperately searching for what she might have forgotten.

The freezers were stocked, the simple menu planned. Dishware, glassware, silverware, condiments had been checked and double-checked. Inspections had been passed, permits and licenses obtained and approved.

"What are we missing?"

"This," he said, going down on one knee and holding out a small velvet box. "I love you, Samantha Appelhoff, and I want this package deal to be permanent. Marry me, Sam."

Sam brought both hands up to her mouth. She looked down at the man before her on bended knee, the man she had come to need more than her next breath. The one looking back at her with pure love in his eyes. The one who always believed in her.

"*Yes*."

He grinned as he slipped the ring onto her finger, then stood up and pulled her into one of those branding, soul-searing kisses she had become addicted to.

"Looks like she said yes," she heard Doc say.

"Thank God," Mad Dog said with feeling.

"About damn time he got around to it." That was from Cage.

"If you two want to move right into the celebratory engagement sex, go right ahead," Heff said, pulling out a chair at the table next to them. "Don't mind us. Oh, look, champagne. Church, where'd you put those glasses?"

Steve reluctantly broke their kiss and sighed. "So much for our moment."

Sam laughed softly. "Our moment was perfect."

Here, in the arms of the man she loved, surrounded by her new family, she couldn't imagine anything better.

"Here," Church said, holding out an envelope to her.

"What's this?"

"Good wishes from the Callaghans on the official opening."

"The Callaghans?" Sam mused, extracting the card. "Do I know them?"

"No, but they know you. Ian Callaghan was the

one who helped us out last spring."

Sam didn't have to ask what Church was talking about. She knew Cage had been dealing with someone with extraordinary clearance and data mining skills. Now, she had a name to add to her list of nightly whispered thank-yous.

"He sent that, too."

Sam looked over at the massive crate Church pointed to, near the general service and delivery entrance. It had arrived earlier that afternoon, but since it was addressed to Church, she hadn't opened it.

"What is it?"

He grinned. "See for yourself."

With Steve by her side, she walked over and lifted up the lid.

"Fire extinguishers?" she asked.

"Yep," Church said with a wry grin. "Four dozen of them, all kinds, everything from kitchen to electric fires. He's already hooked us up with the latest in digital fire and smoke detectors, too."

"Warped sense of humor or genuine concern?"

"Probably a little of both."

"Fits right in then."

"He and his will always have a place here, should they need it," Church agreed.

Sam accepted the glass of champagne and raised her hand in toast with the others.

"To family," Church said.

"To friends," Steve added.

"To us," Sam said, looking at each and every one of them. At the man she loved, now her fiancé. At these strong, good-hearted men who had become like brothers. It was amazing what they had accomplished together, and the future held unlimited promise. "To *all* of us."

Ready for Heff?

Best Laid Plans (Heff's story) is the next book in the Sanctuary series. Read on for a preview...

Sandy

"Well, uh, thanks." Sandy Summers cringed as the words came out of her mouth. They sounded so lame. What were women supposed to say in a situation like this? She wasn't well-versed in one-night-stand etiquette. But she had just had the best sex of her life, so she'd felt compelled to say *something*.

Propped up on one elbow and looking sexier than any man should, he watched her, his dark green eyes glistening as that glittering diamond stud in his ear caught the light. Long, glossy hair draped over his cheek and neck, as inky black as the intricate tats that adorned his tan, muscled arms and torso. His lips quirked up in a roguish half-smile, all the more devastating now that she knew exactly the kind of pleasure those lips were capable of.

"You're welcome."

His voice, like everything else about him, screamed dark, decadent, and delicious. The personification of sin—that was what he was. Sin and pleasure and a wellspring of guaranteed orgasms. In the last three hours, he'd given her four. His fingers were as skilled as his tongue, and the way he moved those hips …

Heat rushed into her face while simultaneously blossoming in the still-tingling region between her thighs. His grin widened, as if he knew exactly what she was thinking. Maybe he did. Or maybe he was just really, *really* good at reading body language. He had known exactly where to touch, when to lick, and how to bite to take her right to the edge over and over …

Stop it, she silently commanded, pushing the words down toward her rebellious regions, the ones clamoring for just one more. *You've had more than enough.*

She jabbed one leg into her jeans, a physical manifestation of her frustration as the haze of post-orgasmic bliss began to dissipate. He continued to watch her, still and predatory and, for the moment, satisfied. Although, given his remarkable endurance and recovery time, that wouldn't last long. She needed to leave before he coaxed her back into that bed and reminded her why she'd thrown caution to the wind in the first place.

Not an easy thing to do when he was looking at her like that.

She spied her panties on the chair in the corner where they must have landed after he tossed them over his shoulder. An image of him grinning in smug triumph as he'd removed them slowly and with such deliberate intent, his eyes burning with lust, had her nipples hardening again. Apparently, he wasn't the only one with a quick recovery time.

She snatched them up with a huff and unceremoniously crammed them into her pocket before her traitorous body won the stay-versus-go tug-of-war with her mind. She didn't need to be putting on damp panties. The trip back to her place was short enough to go commando.

He made no move to stop her, which was her saving grace. He just lay there, the sheet draped over the bottom half of his happy trail, watching her with the lazy interest of a man who had gotten off a few times too. No false platitudes or disingenuous sentiments. They both knew what this was— namely, *nothing*—and they were completely, totally, absolutely, one hundred percent on the same page about that.

She pulled the shirt over her head, grabbed her purse, and turned to look back at him one last time. She sensed, more than saw, a wariness lurking beneath that smoldering stare. As if he was expecting her to suggest something more. Like maybe grabbing a drink sometime or a request for a repeat.

She wouldn't. In less than a week, she'd be starting her new life, and he'd be nothing but a lovely memory tucked away in her personal, private spank bank.

Sandy offered him a genuine smile. "Bye."

His eyes flickered, widening slightly in either surprise or disappointment—she wasn't sure which.

"Bye."

Wham, bam, thank you, stud.

Thanks for reading Steve and Sam's story

You didn't have to pick this book, but you did. Thank you!

If you liked this story, then please consider posting a review online! It's really easy, only takes a few minutes, and makes a huge difference to independent authors who don't have the mega-budgets of the big-time publishers behind them.

Do you like free books? How about gift cards?

Sign up for my newsletter today! You'll not only get advance notice of new releases, sales, giveaways, contests, fun facts, and other great things each month, you'll also get a free book just for signing up *and* be automatically entered for a chance to win a gift card every month, simply for reading it!

Go to **abbiezandersromance.com** and click on **Subscribe** to get started today!

Thanks again, and may all of your ever-afters be happy ones!

 Abbie

Also by Abbie Zanders

Contemporary Romance – Callaghan Brothers

Plan your visit to Pine Ridge, Pennsylvania and fall in love with the Callaghans

- 📖 Dangerous Secrets
- 📖 First and Only
- 📖 House Calls
- 📖 Seeking Vengeance
- 📖 Guardian Angel
- 📖 Beyond Affection
- 📖 Having Faith
- 📖 Bottom Line
- 📖 Forever Mine
- 📖 Two of a Kind
- 📖 Not Quite Broken

Contemporary Romance – Connelly Cousins

Drive across the river to Birch Falls and spend some time with the Connelly Cousins

- 📖 Celina
- 📖 Jamie
- 📖 Johnny
- 📖 Michael

Contemporary Romance – Covendale Series

If you like humor and snark in your romance, add a stop in Covendale

- 📖 Five Minute Man
- 📖 All Night Woman
- 📖 Seizing Mack

Contemporary Romance – Sanctuary

More small town romance with former military heroes you can't help but love

- 📖 Protecting Sam
- 📖 Best Laid Plans
- 📖 Shadow of Doubt
- 📖 Nick UnCaged
- 📖 Organically Yours
- 📖 Finding Home (Long Road Home crossover)
- 📖 Prodigal Son

More Contemporary Romance

- 📖 The Realist

- 📖 Celestial Desire
- 📖 Letting Go
- 📖 SEAL Out of Water (Silver SEALs)
- 📖 Rockstar Romeo (Cocky Hero Club)
- 📖 Finding Home (The Long Road Home)
- 📖 Cast in Shadow (Shadow SEALs)

Cerasino Family Novellas

Short, sweet romance to put a smile on your face

- 📖 Just For Me
- 📖 Just For Him
- 📖 Just For Her
- 📖 Just For Us

Time Travel Romance

Travel between present day NYC and 15th century Scotland in these stand-alone but related titles

- 📖 Maiden in Manhattan
- 📖 Raising Hell in the Highlands

Paranormal Romance – Mythic Series

Welcome to Mythic, an idyllic community all kinds of Extraordinaries call home.

- 📖 Faerie Godmother
- 📖 Fallen Angel
- 📖 The Oracle at Mythic
- 📖 Wolf Out of Water

More Paranormal Romance

- 📖 Vampire, Unaware
- 📖 Black Wolfe's Mate (written as Avelyn McCrae)
- 📖 Going Nowhere
- 📖 The Jewel
- 📖 Close Encounters of the Sexy Kind
- 📖 Rock Hard
- 📖 Immortal Dreams
- 📖 Rehabbing the Beast (written as Avelyn McCrae)
- 📖 More Than Mortal

Howls Romance

Classic romance with a furry twist

- 📖 Falling for the Werewolf
- 📖 A Very Beary Christmas

📖 Going Polar

Historical/Medieval Romance

📖 A Warrior's Heart (written as Avelyn McCrae)

About the Author

Abbie Zanders loves to read and write romance in all forms; she is quite obsessive, really. Her ultimate fantasy is to spend all of her free time doing both, preferably in a secluded mountain cabin overlooking a pristine lake, though a private beach on a lush tropical island works, too. Sharing her work with others of similar mind is a dream come true. She promises her readers two things: no cliffhangers, and there will always be a happy ending. Beyond that, you never know…

Made in the USA
Columbia, SC
07 May 2024